By Naomi Novik

The Summer War
Buried Deep and Other Stories
Uprooted
Spinning Silver

THE SCHOLOMANCE

A Deadly Education
The Last Graduate
The Golden Enclaves

TEMERAIRE

His Majesty's Dragon
Throne of Jade
Black Powder War
Empire of Ivory
Victory of Eagles
Tongues of Serpents
Crucible of Gold
Blood of Tyrants

THE SUMMER WAR

THE
SUMMER
WAR

NAOMI NOVIK

NEW YORK

Del Rey
An imprint of Random House
A division of Penguin Random House LLC
1745 Broadway, New York, NY 10019
randomhousebooks.com
penguinrandomhouse.com

Hardcover ISBN 978-0-593-98470-3

Ebook ISBN 978-0-593-98471-0

Printed in the United States of America on acid-free paper

9 8 7 6 5 4 3 2 1

First Edition

BOOK TEAM: Production editor: Michelle Daniel •
Managing editor: Paul Gilbert • Production manager: Angela McNally •
Copy editor: Laura Jorstad • Proofreaders: Jill Falzoi, Lawrence Krauser,
Christoper Ross

Book design by Susan Turner

The authorized representative in the EU for product safety
and compliance is Penguin Random House Ireland,
Morrison Chambers, 32 Nassau Street, Dublin D02 YH68,
Ireland. https://eu-contact.penguin.ie

THE SUMMER WAR

CELIA WAS TWELVE YEARS OLD ON THE DAY SHE CURSED HER brother. She had two brothers, but she didn't count Roric, the middle child, because no one did. He was a thin sour weasel who glared at her whenever he saw her, and almost not a real son of the house. His mother—there had been three wives in a row, one to get each child—had just been a temporary mistress, common-born; Father hadn't meant to marry her at all. Everyone knew that her son didn't really matter.

But Celia's oldest brother, Argent, whose mother had been the daughter of an earl, mattered in every way there was. He was Father's heir and the best knight in the world, so everyone said. Argent was very handsome, too, with black hair that curled and blue-grey eyes, and he'd played with Celia ever since she'd been born. He'd been trained at home, instead of being sent to the king's circle, and she'd run after him as soon as she could run.

The summer war had been over since before Celia had been born—Father had won it for Prosper, which was how he had become Grand Duke Veris—and now only the summer games took place instead, but Argent trained just as hard as if his life depended on it. Each day Celia hurried through her work so she could go sit in the hall that faced the training yard, even though it was cold in winter and hot in summer, and watch him at his endless sword and javelin drills and riding exercises. Sometimes he would toss her shrieking in delight up into the air, and run around the yard carrying her on his back, and he dressed her up and braided her hair like a doll, and when she was older, he taught her how to dance and ride and shoot a bow. She never got very good with the bow, but he was patient, and even when all her arrows ended up scattered flat over the ground, at least ten feet away from the target, he only laughed and said, "Don't worry, Celie; if anyone ever tries to hurt you, I'll be there to stop them." And she said, "Do you promise?" and he said, "On my honor, my lady," and bowed to her deeply, just like a knight out of a summer story.

When Argent turned nineteen, Father armed him in fine steel and let him go to the summer games, and almost at once every song-spinner who came to Castle Todholme—and many of them came, because they all hoped to get a bit of story from Father, or at least to be able to say, "Grand Duke Veris, who lately hosted me at Todholme," the next time they told one of the stories about the end of the summer war—began to say that he was the best knight in the world. He had won three challenges against summer knights on his first day, and they'd started quarreling amongst themselves for the right to face him.

Celia would rather have had him back home, but it was a consolation to have such stories about him. And they pleased her father, who was very hard to please. She could only please him herself with courtesy, if guests came and she hosted for him like a great lady, so their cups were always filled and the conversation never flagged, and they told her father that she would grace the tables of a king. Then when they left he would tell her, "You behaved well," and give her some money to buy a new dress, and she would use half the money for the dress, and the rest to buy a book full of summer stories. But her father was even more pleased when people told him that Argent was the best knight in the world.

Summer in Prosper lasted almost five months, longer than in the rest of the mortal world, because they shared a border with the Summer Lands. They could grow an extra crop each year, and make wine and silk and sugar, so it had made them much richer than all their other neighbors. But that year Celia grudged every minute of sun and summer rains, and flicked away every gleambug that she saw, just in case the superstition about them getting annoyed and ending summer early might be true. She was so happy the day she woke up with the wind blowing too-sharp through her bed hangings and heard the servants putting up the autumn walls outside.

But Argent didn't come home right away. After two weeks, a song-spinner brought them the news that he'd been an honored guest at the closing feast, and Summer Prince Elithyon had given him a magnificent gift: "'For the champion Sir Argent, a blade to match his virtues,'" the spinner said grandly, quoting the prince, "'silver his name, gold his grace, and steel his courage,'" and said that it had been woven of all three metals together by a great summerling spell-smith.

It was two more weeks after that song-spinner had been and gone, with a fat purse and a firsthand account of one of Father's battles to reward him for rushing to bring them the news, before Argent finally came home. The weather had truly turned; when autumn did come to Prosper, it came with a vengeance. Celia had moved to her rooms in the winter towers, and that night she was kneeling at the windowsill with her candle already blown out so her nurse wouldn't lecture her about staying up again. She saw him coming along the road in the moonlight, and she knew it was him by his riding, even though he was alone when he should have had an escort of her father's men, and he went to the small gate by the stables to be let in.

She didn't even stop to put on slippers or a gown over her shift; she dashed down the stairs to the mezzanine landing, and saw him standing below in the hall. She was going to call down to him, but then she didn't, hesitating. He looked different and somehow strange. He'd grown, and was wearing new armor, and his face was very hard and beautiful and still. She heard old Unter tell him that Father was in the library, so instead she crept along the mezzanine, shadowing them as they walked to the next hall and peeking over at Argent some more all the way, hoping he would stop seeming strange to her.

But in the library, as Father rose to greet him—he was even smiling a little, more emotion than he almost ever let himself show—Argent waited by the door, holding it open until Unter, disappointed, went back out instead of staying with them for the welcoming cup. Then Argent went and stood before Father, and he didn't take the cup when Father held it out.

Father stood holding it another moment, and then the same hard stillness came into his face, too. It was familiar there, though. He put the cup down. "Well?" he said.

Argent said, "I'm not staying." He paused a moment and then said, "Do you remember when you took me to the town court, when I was a boy?" Father didn't answer, but peering down at his face through the narrow bars of the mezzanine railing, Celia could tell that he knew exactly what Argent was talking about. Argent didn't wait for him to say anything. "You almost never went there at all. That was work for your magistrates to do, not you yourself. But that day we went, and you judged the first case yourself. They'd—taken two men together."

Drawing away a little from the railing, Celia huddled

herself in small and close, arms wrapped tightly around her knees. She knew what Argent was talking about, and she also knew she didn't want to hear any more of what he was going to say. She wanted to leave, and she couldn't bear to leave.

"One of them was the son of one of your men at arms. The other one . . . I think he was a merchant's son. I remember them begging you for mercy. You didn't give it. You ordered them caned on the spot, right there in the court. I remember every blow, the screaming. And afterwards, you stripped them of their names, to spare their families the shame of them. And you ordered them taken to the border of your lands and thrown out, never to return, on pain of death." Argent said it all so calmly, so steadily, like giving a patrol report, one dull thing after another, but Celia wept for him, her mouth pressed tight to keep the sound in, tears leaking down her face and falling hot on her shift. Her belly was aching.

"I was only twelve," Argent went on. "I barely even *knew*, yet. I didn't understand what you were trying to do. All I understood was that there was something wrong with me, the same thing that was wrong with them, and you were showing me what it meant. What you had to do about it. And I didn't see anything I could do to stop being wrong, because I hadn't done anything to start. So afterwards, I was only waiting for you to come and take me, to do the same."

Father flinched. The small jerk of movement was loud as bells. Father never moved except when he meant to; he never fidgeted or twitched or stirred except to say something, even just with a raised brow or a tilt of his head, and then he always meant to say it. But he hadn't meant to flinch.

"I was so *terrified*," Argent was saying, with an odd sound of wonder in his voice, as if he couldn't believe the scale of his own fear even now. "Nothing has ever frightened me since. Everyone calls me brave, but it's only that nothing else comes close enough to that fear. I lived with it for three days and three nights, *waiting*, until I couldn't bear it any longer. And then I went into the gardens and I took nightshade, which Father Mullin had told us never to eat, because it was poison, and I ate a handful of it. I didn't want to die, I was afraid of dying, but I thought it would be better to be dead. Do you remember? I was very ill after."

Yes, Celia wanted to whisper. *Yes, I remember.* It was a vague, half-forgotten terror in her mind: the time when Argent had almost died. She'd been five years old, and she'd already loved him more than anyone else in the world. She remembered the hushed voices and the priest and the physician coming and going and talking, and her father simply vanishing out of the world, into Argent's room, for three days and nights, until they had been told that Argent would live.

"When I woke, you were there," Argent said. "And I thought you'd come to take me." Father flinched again. "I remember begging you: *please, don't*. I swore I wouldn't ever. I couldn't tell you *what* I wouldn't do, because I didn't really know. But I would have said anything, promised anything. And then," his voice dropped almost to a whisper, so low that Celia could barely hear it, and only because there wasn't another sound; if Father breathed, she couldn't tell, "you kissed my brow. You told me to hush. You said that everything would be well, and I only needed to rest and get my strength back. It felt like—a pardon. A miracle. I was—*grateful*."

He was silent after, for a long time, and Father didn't speak either. He didn't say a word at all. "I do understand, now, what you meant to do," Argent said finally. "You didn't mean to frighten me to death. You only meant to teach me, so I'd never forget, what I wasn't allowed to have. To *want*. And it worked well. I did understand, afterwards, that the only thing I could want was the sword. That if I wanted anything else . . ." He didn't finish. He paused a moment, and then he went on, a little unsteadily, "So from this day, I will never again use your name, to spare you my shame. And I return to you the sword you let me carry, so long as I was fit to be your son."

He had two swords on his belt, one on either side, which Celia had half noticed. He took one off, the sword Father had given him when he'd ridden away to war, in its sheath of leather and silver, and he laid it on the table. The other one he wore had a narrow hilt made all of metal, three bands that gleamed in different colors of gold and steel and silver, woven together like a braid. "And I will go now, away beyond the border of your lands, and never return again. Farewell, Your Grace."

He turned and walked out of the library, and left the door open behind him. Father still didn't say anything. He didn't tell Argent to stop or to wait, and didn't tell him he was sorry. He only stood behind the table, looking down at the sword, and his face was as blank as an unwritten page.

But Celia crept along the mezzanine back to the hall, and then as fast as she could, she ran down the stair and through the inner court, bare feet slapping on the stones and the wind biting through her shift. She just made it out into the stable yard as Argent reached his horse, tied up and waiting, and she called out desperately, "Argent!"

He stopped. His hands were on his saddle, and for a moment she almost thought he would just finish mounting and go, that he wouldn't even answer. Then he did turn to look at her, slowly. But his face was still so hard and strange, and she halted in the middle of the yard halfway to him, forlorn. He stared at her almost as if he didn't know her. "Celia," he said slowly, and it was—*polite;* he might as well have said *Lady Celia* instead, the way the guests and the servants did.

She couldn't say anything back to that. She only stood

and stared at him dumbly, and the prickling tears started out of her eyes and came down her face. But he moved a little when he saw them, a small jerking that made him look more like himself. "Celie," he said again, a little wavering, and then he was Argent again, not just a stranger with his face.

"I've been waiting for you to come home," she said, half pleading, half accusatory. "I've been waiting all summer."

He said slowly, "I'm sorry," but she knew at once, with a terrible hollowness like someone had scooped out a space under her ribs, that it was just more politeness. He didn't mean it truly.

"No, you're not," she said, barely above a whisper, her throat tight. "It doesn't really matter to you. *I* don't. If I mattered, you couldn't go away forever, without even saying anything." It was horrible to know that she didn't matter to him, but she saw it too clearly not to know. He hadn't given her a single thought. He'd only come to take revenge on Father and go away again. The only reason she even knew he'd come at all was because *she'd* been up. Waiting. She asked helplessly, even knowing it was stupid and would only make it worse, "*Why* don't I matter?"

"You *do*," he said, and she wanted to believe him, but then he said, "Celie, I can't stay, it's his castle—" and she lost her temper and ran at him and hit him with both her fists, high on his chest.

"Shut up!" she said. "Shut up, you liar." He caught her wrists, holding her hands away from him so she wouldn't bruise them on his armor, but she glared up at him past them. "Do you think I'm stupid? What if I say I want to go too? What if I ask you to take me away with you, so I don't have to marry that fat old duke?" He stared back, caught without an answer. "I'm *not* stupid. Now that you've cast off your name, you don't owe anything to Father, to anyone. You're going to take your magic sword and go have adventures, and all the boys you like, and you're casting me off, too, because I'd only get in your way," she said, savagely, and was glad to see Argent flinch, the same way that Father had flinched. She was burning with anger, more because he'd tried to lie to her than anything else. It was bad enough that he *was* casting her off; it was bad enough that he didn't care. He didn't need to tell her insultingly stupid lies on top of it.

"Celie," he said, his voice cracking. "No—that's not—" But that *was* it, no matter how hard he pretended it wasn't, and when she stared at him and refused to go along with the lie, he sputtered to a halt. But then he tried *again*, like a mouse scurrying desperately in another direction, trying to find another hole. He said, "I'm not going to be safe. I'm going to the Summer Lands—"

"Stop it!" she said. "If you won't even be honest to me, if you won't let me matter even that littlest bit, just *go*!" She jerked her hands free and stepped back and away from him. "Go to the Summer Lands! Go ride a shaihul, fight a dragon, be the greatest knight who ever lived. Just see if it makes you happy! I hope you meet a hundred beautiful summerling boys and none of them love you. I hope no one else is ever stupid enough to love you again!"

She ran away from him and back inside the stable door, so he wouldn't see her crying, but as soon as she was over the threshold and out of sight, she burst into a huge sob that shook her whole body when she gulped it down painfully to keep the sound in, and another one wanted to come right after it. She bent over her aching belly and then just sank down on her knees in the dirty corridor and crawled herself over to huddle against the wall next to the mucking shovels and pitchforks. She pressed her head against her knees and her mouth against her folded arms to keep quiet, listening as hard as she could until she heard the horrible sound of the horse's hooves clattering as Argent rode away forever, and then she could let the rage and misery come burning out of her in tears.

She wanted to believe, afterwards, that she wouldn't have said the curse if she'd known that it would work. She loved Argent more than she hated him, even in the moment. But oh—she wanted so much for the words to hurt him a little, to stick in his head like a pebble in his shoe, so he *would* have to take her, some part of her, away with him for just a little while, until he cast even that off and found himself some summer lord to fall in love with, in their courts of endless green, and lived happily ever after for a hundred years, likely forgetting the whole mortal world and her along with it.

Celia had been taught over and over not to ill-wish. Father reminded her often, to make her proud, that she was of the bloodline of the great Witch-Queen Selina, who had founded Prosper's line of kings. His third wife, her mother, had been the bastard sister of the king, and the great tapestry in their dining hall, which Father had commissioned after her birth, showed Selina's Seventh Wyrd: Queen Selina standing stern and beautiful on a mountaintop, looking down on the army of the shadow-lords, and the summerlings and the mortal armies of Prosper united behind her, about to be drowned in darkness.

And Celia also had a book that showed Selina's First Wyrd: the illustration of Selina holding her hands out to her parents, her mouth open in a wail of horror and grief, while they stretched their own out to her in return, with stone twining itself up around their bodies like a winding sheet. Celia had read it over and over; she'd played private games in the gardens, whispering pretend spells, imagining that when she became a woman, she would be the one, the next sorceress of Prosper.

But more than sixty girls descended of Witch-Queen Selina had been born over the long years since her death without another sorceress flowering in the line, and Celia didn't feel anything like a woman at the moment. She felt like the opposite—a stupid angry little child, deceived and hurt and crying in a corner, trying to nurse her wounded heart and pride. Even after Argent rode away, Celia still didn't know that she'd cursed him. She didn't even know that her courses had started.

She sat in the dark weeping with her head against her knees, thinking the cold and wet and pain were only sorrow, until one of the grooms came yawning on his way to the stables and thought he saw a servant girl in a shift crying and said in rough kindness, "Here, lambkin, what's the blubbing for? Someone's hurt ye?"

She jerked her head up and stared at him as he came closer with his candle, and he went pale as a bleached sheet and said, "Gods, milady!" and turned and shouted down the hall, "Here! Here's milady hurt! Rouse up the house, come quick, go tell the duke!" and he ran to her even as a bell started clanging.

He knelt and put the candle down and reached halfway out with his hands, not quite daring to touch her, full of worry. "Where is't, milady, where are you hurt?" he asked, and she looked down at herself and in the candlelight she saw the blood, bright crimson spreading like a terrible flower through the soft white linen of her shift, and felt the dreadful chill of power spreading through her body with it. She stared at it, and then she realized what she'd done. She screamed just as three guards came running from the gate, and they all fell down and covered their heads in terror as their swords turned to glass and shattered in their hands.

THE SUMMER WAR HAD GONE for a hundred years before Father had finally won it. There hadn't been endless fighting all of that time; the summerlings only ever attacked during summer, and sometimes they forgot about the war and didn't turn up for years at a time, and all the king's men just sat in the border keeps along the Meanwhile River, bored and drinking and sweltering in summer heat. But Prosper still had to have an army ready every year, because every so often the summerlings *did* remember about the Betrayal, and as soon as they did, they all blazed up with rage and came storming across the border, swords out for every man, woman, and child in Prosper.

The summerlings had been something like their friends before the war. For as long as anyone had lived in Prosper—or at least as long as anyone knew about—each year the summerlings had come across the Green Bridge to trade "silk and leather and wine and cake for beautiful things of summer make," as it went in the song. Summerlings couldn't be bothered to grow crops or tend animals, but they made things no mortal could: enchanted glass as clear as water, arms of hardened gold and silver, jewels that glowed with cool light. They'd fought together against the shadowlords, and after Witch-Queen Selina and the Summer King had died winning the final battle against them, Summer Prince Elithyon had given his sister in marriage to Selina's son Sherdan, the new king of Prosper.

But the summerlings weren't mortal. They lived in the simplicity of grand towering stories filled with magic and endless high beauty, and for them pride and love were tangled so close together that they couldn't pry them apart. During the wedding feast, Princess Eislaing saw King Sherdan look at song-spinner Minata as she sang, and she instantly realized that not only hadn't her new husband fallen in desperate love with her on first sight the way he should have, he was in love with someone else—an ordinary mortal woman, who wasn't radiantly beautiful and didn't even sing perfectly on-key. So as soon as the feast ended, Eislaing went straight up to the highest tower of the royal castle and threw herself off. Her story had gone all wrong, and she couldn't see anything else to do.

Prince Elithyon and all the summerlings had loved their princess as the greatest treasure of their realm. To them, King Sherdan and the horrible people of Prosper, who hadn't appreciated the impossibly glorious gift they'd been given, had driven her to a hideous death. The only possible response was to avenge her. And as far as Elithyon was concerned, that was going to take the blood of everyone in the entire kingdom.

So he'd started the summer war, and for a long time, no one had been able to end it. Prosper couldn't invade them in return. If an army of mortal men marched into the Summer Lands, half of the soldiers wandered out again the next day, fifty years older, and the other half wandered out again ten years later not having aged a day and having forgotten who they were. The lords and generals came out gibbering mad. Only heroes and songspinners could go into the Summer Lands, and half of those didn't come back either—some because they'd died heroically, and some because a summerling had seduced them and persuaded them to stay. Summer lords didn't seem to find anything odd about welcoming individual knights from Prosper into their halls as honored guests, even if they would have slaughtered them without mercy on the other side.

But even on the three occasions when the summerlings had broken through the wall of border keeps and started rampaging through Prosper, razing every town and slaughtering every person in their path, they'd only kept going until autumn. When the leaves started turning colors and falling from the trees, their magic and immortality started fading along with them, and they all panicked and fled pell-mell back to the Summer Lands in terror, abandoning all the ground they'd taken. And then they completely forgot all about autumn until the next time it happened.

So it seemed as though the summer war would just keep going forever and ever, and everyone in Prosper was just doomed to live under the threat of bursts of slaughter, until Father arrived on the border and changed everything, because he started winning.

Father always knew the right thing to do. He was born the son of a poor landless knight from the backwater of Prosper, the northern mountain country, all the way on the other side from the Summer Lands. His only inheritance was some patchy armor, a badly sized sword, a thin horse, and a lowly position with the local earl. But when the king sent one of his periodic demands for soldiers for the summer war, Father asked the earl to let him have the command. The request was granted with alacrity; no one lucky enough to live in the north wanted to be sent down to the summer war.

The strategy that Prosper had relied on for more than a hundred years by then was simple. The king maintained a ring of stone-walled forts all along the border. The forts were hideously uncomfortable, each one built of a few winter towers, naked with no autumn halls or shady summer gardens outside, and joined together by stone walls with almost no openings, except for one entrance just big enough to ride a single horse through at a time. They were oven-hot when the sun was out, full of greenish mold and mosquitoes when the summer rains fell, and often both at the same time. But they were hard to take without siege equipment, which the summerlings almost never managed to finish building.

The men hunkered miserably down inside the forts and the commanders sent out their most gifted knights and well-arrayed companies to offer the summerlings individual challenges and small battles, just often enough to keep them from getting bored and organizing a more concerted advance. It worked reasonably well. Usually only two or three forts got overrun each season, and at worst only a few villages and towns got butchered before autumn came: acceptable losses.

Father's assigned fort was an especially uncomfortable one: only three towers, all too stubby to risk a window bigger than an arrow-slit even on the topmost floors, and the stone walls were uneasily low and thin. The previous summer's defenders had prudently dug a ditch around the whole thing to make a bit more of an obstacle, which was already filling up with water as the rains began, and stank to high heaven, since all the castle's waste got thrown over the back wall and fell right into it.

But Father didn't sit there waiting to be besieged. Instead, he scouted out the nearest ford over the river, and when the spring mists began to clear, he took his men out and hid halfway along the way. When a small company of summer knights rode by on their way to besiege him—a shining troop in their armor of hardened silver, singing in clear voices about the joy of death in battle—he and his men threw muck and shit and small rocks at them from cover, shouting insults. The summerlings charged after them at once and fell straight into a prepared pit trap, where Father had them ignominiously butchered by a crew of peasants he'd rounded up from the nearest villages, who stood on the edge and stabbed them with spears from a safe distance.

The rest of the summerlings were horrified and outraged, and all the more so when Father sent the nearest summerling lord an insulting message bragging of his victory over them, written crudely on dirty paper. The summer lord immediately gathered a large force of knights to take Father's small and unimportant fort and slaughter everyone in it. The summerlings arrived, overwhelmed the handful of defenders on the gate, stormed into the fort, and were bewildered to find it completely empty. Outside, Father and the rest of his men came out of their hiding places in the nearby brush and threw torches over the walls into the courtyard, which had been drenched with oil and smeared with tar. Nearly four hundred summer knights and a summer lord died, and Father lost less than twenty men.

The king made Father a baron after that, granting him his own lands and a thousand men to command. It wasn't a sincere gesture of appreciation; King Morthimer— Sherdan's great-great-grandson—wasn't pleased to have a hedgeborn knight from the hinterlands showing him up to the common folk, and for that matter mucking around with his tried-and-true strategy. But all the summerlings were going to be out for Father's blood now, so he didn't have long to live, and the king wanted to *look* generous. That was made easier because Father humbly asked for a modest grant of lands neighboring his old backwater home.

Father also asked for a short leave, went back to his former lord, and made his first match: he asked for the hand of the earl's daughter Farria in marriage. The earl was privately indignant at such a request coming from his jumped-up former servant, but he grudgingly agreed, and to a hasty wedding—since, after all, everyone knew Father wasn't going to survive to the autumn, and then his daughter would inherit the conveniently nearby lands.

Before heading back to the front, Father took a chunk of Lady Farria's dowry, bought himself a shield and a banner with a red fox on them, and paid one of the best songwrights in Prosper to write a romantic song calling him Veris the Fox, the poor and clever hedgeborn knight who had fallen in love with his lord's beautiful daughter and had been determined to win her hand, and had outwitted the summerlings and become a hero of the realm to do it. It was wildly popular, and as soon as the summerlings heard it on the border, they immediately forgave Father all his unspeakable crimes against them.

Over the rest of that summer, he proceeded to carry

out an utterly ruthless campaign full of every lie, cheat, and trick he could invent, winning one battle after another. The summerlings sent him the gifts and honors they only bestowed on worthy enemies, and he grew rapidly in popularity on the mortal side of the war as well. The common folk of Prosper perhaps disagreed with their king about just how acceptable the annual losses were.

The next summer, the king gave Father the command of the aptly named Fort Resignation, a six-tower castle on the leading edge of the border that had been sacked by the summerlings more than twenty times over the course of the war, and granted him another thousand men, which would have been more generous if the castle hadn't needed at bare minimum a garrison twice as large. Father promptly sent song-spinners out to ten different summerling lords on the border nearby to sing them a song about how the single most valiant summer lord would be the one who took Fort Resignation from Veris the Fox. The instant the mists opened, all of them made straight for the castle. When they were a few days out, Father held a parley with each of them and said apologetically that of course he welcomed their challenge, but he'd already accepted a challenge from the next one over, and couldn't face anyone else until that one was defeated.

The summer lords proceeded to spend half the summer fighting one another savagely for the right to face Father, who meanwhile spent the same time building a much more secure inner fortification out of just one of the towers, and undermining the rest of the walls and turning the courtyard into a bog of quicksand. When the last three surviving summer lords finally worked out that they'd been tricked and agreed to join forces to besiege and take the castle, Father waited for a summer thunderstorm, then collapsed the walls outward onto them, killing half their force. Then he immediately hailed them with a blizzard of small pebbles: he'd recruited boys from all the villages nearby to come with their slingshots, and they were lining every nook and cranny of the inner walls. Half blinded with rain and hailing pebbles, the summerlings charged over the fallen walls and straight into the quicksand, where many of them drowned in the mud struggling to get out, and the rest became easy targets for arrows and spears.

When the skies cleared, the much-reduced remnant of the summerling force besieged the inner tower, seething. Father wasn't there anymore. He'd slipped out through a tunnel during the thunderstorm along with most of his men, leaving only a small garrison to hold the tower. He snuck along to the next border keep, which was also under siege, and fired an arrow over the walls with a song for the men inside to sing, about how Veris the Fox had tricked the summerling lords who now didn't have enough men to take him out of his tower. The summerlings besieging that keep all rode off to join the siege on what was left of Father's castle, and Father rode in and told the knight commanding the keep to come join him.

He did the same to another three keeps, then rode back to his castle with a total of five thousand men, quietly encircled the large summerling camp around the tower, and waited until the summerlings launched their next assault, hundreds of them all launching themselves valiantly up the extremely tall walls and over the top. Inside the tower, his remaining men took down the bracing that was holding up those walls and fled out through the tunnel as the tower came crumbling down, and in the confusion, Father attacked and slaughtered the entire summerling force.

He then marched his men—they were all firmly his men by then—to the next besieged border keep, killed the summerlings there, absorbed the garrison into his force, and kept going. By the end of the summer, he'd lifted the sieges on seventeen keeps and had killed tens of thousands of summerlings. The king grimly made *him* an earl in his own right, gave him still more lands in the north, and sent him home to rule them before he could become too powerful.

Argent was a healthy and promising one-year-old boy by then, toddling around. Lady Farria died along with a stillborn girl the next year, but Father didn't mourn very long. Shortly afterwards, her father the earl and his only son both died in a slightly questionable accident. Father promptly claimed the earl's lands in Argent's name, doubling the size of his estate, and started negotiating to marry the sole heiress of another earldom next to his, which would have made him the greatest landowner in the north and a significant power in the realm.

That was when his mistress got pregnant. Mistress Perilla was just a common-born song-spinner that he'd picked precisely because she could be quietly packed off without offending anyone as soon as he could make a match with another noblewoman. Father still had no intention of marrying her, but when the local soothsayer came for the usual visit and put his hands on her belly, instead of just delivering the pro forma prophecy of good fortune and an easy birth, the man's eyes went all white and he told Father that she would bear him a son who would be useful to his other children, and hold the door open for power to come flowing into his house. Another man might have tried to stick to his plan anyway, but Father was too sensible not to respect a prophecy. He married her at once.

There hadn't been any summer attacks during those two years, but not long after the wedding, the summerlings appeared for the next season in massive force, united under the direct command of Summer Prince Elithyon himself. Instead of besieging the border forts, he brought them all across the Green Bridge, smashed through the defenses there, and took the royal road straight for the capital of Prosper. He didn't even let his lords and knights sack the castles and towns and villages on the way, unless someone offered them battle, which very few people did. The current royal palace—it had been built after the start of the summer war—was almost as far away from the border as you could get and still be in the heartlands of Prosper, but it looked very much like he was still going to make it there before autumn.

King Morthimer decided that, on reflection, he preferred having a dangerously powerful lord at his back to being slowly roasted alive on a spit or sliced into a thousand pieces one at a time with thin sharp wires—the summerlings grew very elaborate when they caught anyone of high rank to kill, as a gesture of respect, and they'd never yet had the chance to kill a king of Prosper—and yelled for help.

Father rode down from the north at breakneck speed to assume command of the army, and then proceeded not to do anything with it except wait. He did send men down the royal road to burn all the bridges and fill all the fords with caltrops to slow down the summerling advance, and also sent Elithyon several cartloads of sparkling wine and sugar candy as a token of respect, which delayed him by almost another week—the summerlings hadn't had much of either during the war, and they immediately stopped to have a very enthusiastic feast—but otherwise Father just stayed camped right outside the capital until the summer army arrived, three solid weeks before the weather would turn at the earliest. The king was feeling extremely anxious by then, but he also didn't have any better options.

Father met the summerlings on open ground right before the capital, at the head of a gloriously arrayed force—knights in full plate, flags and banners waving, horns blowing, presenting exactly the sort of dream of battle that every summer knight and lord longed to fight in—and marched straight towards them, with his own flags, emblazoned with red foxes, streaming at the front. Knowing who he was facing, the Summer Prince immediately split up his forces and sent companies into the woods on either side, trying futilely to find the extra men that Father had surely hidden somewhere, and backed away over the field until his army had almost reached the previous ford, putting themselves on much worse ground than they'd had and disordering their ranks.

While Prince Elithyon kept hunting for the secret trap that didn't exist, Father sent dozens of knights riding forward to offer direct challenges of one-on-one swordfights. It was too much of a temptation to the summerlings, already sullen about the lack of battle along the way; the front ranks of their army started breaking up completely as summer knights and lords rushed forward to accept the challenges, in some cases quarreling amongst themselves about who got to have the fight. The summerlings won most of the duels, of course, but before they could return to their lines, Father blew the horns and sent off a massive flight of arrows, followed by a cavalry charge that smashed through the large gaps they'd left. Thousands of summer knights were slaughtered en masse in a perfectly straightforward battle, and Elithyon had to order a desperate retreat over the river.

Elithyon meant to regroup, but he was out of time on the clock he hadn't remembered was running. Just as he finally got his army back into order, the rains stopped, the first cold autumn day blew through, and seven leaves turned yellow and fell off a tree in his camp. All his summerlings broke in horror and fled south down the royal road as fast as they could go, leaving him stranded in the middle of Prosper with only the tiny devoted core of the summer guard, and Father's army on the march towards them.

But King Morthimer, perhaps fearing what Father might decide to do with the army *after* he'd disposed of the Summer Prince, intervened at that point. He sent an envoy to Elithyon and offered him peace terms. Every envoy who'd been sent to the summerlings over the previous century had been sent back in pieces, with their head enchanted to declare the summerlings' eternal determination to kill them all, but this time a chastened Elithyon finally agreed to negotiate, and at the Green Bridge he swore an oath of gold and silver to never again invade Prosper before he too fled the changing season.

And by the time Father rode back into the capital after his great victory, with frenzied crowds cheering wildly along every street, a messenger was waiting to tell him that the prophecy had come true: his second son, Roric, had been born, and his inconvenient commoner wife had conveniently died in the process, leaving the now Grand Duke Veris free to ask the king for the hand of his baseborn sister.

The king agreed with much relief: he'd been expecting a demand for the hand of his actual daughter, despite her young years, with real concerns about the future of his own son, Crown Prince Gorthan, who was only ten at the time. Father wasn't having to commission song-spinners to get songs written about him anymore, and it was a settled matter among the common folk that he was the savior of the realm.

But Father had known exactly what to do then, too. He'd known that putting himself too close to the throne—or on it—would stir up enormous resentment among the great lords of the realm, who were already resentful of him, and make him a target of conspiracy. So instead he asked only for Lady Cecily, and as a dowry, the great royal castle of Todholme along with its rich lands, to make an appropriate home for her. He brought his new wife and his two young sons there, and settled in to get what he very much hoped would be a daughter of royal blood.

He meant to marry that girl to the grand duke who was his new neighbor, and breed up grandchildren who'd be rich and of ancient lineage and have just enough of a claim to the throne so that when Crown Prince Gorthan grew up and had children, he would accept a betrothal to one of them for his own heir, and give Father a royal princess to be Argent's wife. And at that point, the fortunes of the crown would be tied to his so securely that Gorthan would just do whatever Father told him.

SO THAT HAD BEEN FATHER's well-laid plan: a steady two-decade conquest of the throne by a penniless boy from the back of nowhere, which he meant to accomplish without fighting a single battle against anyone in the kingdom, and putting an end to the wasteful summer war while he was at it. He didn't care if he wore the crown or not; he only wanted to put himself in charge. Mostly, Celia felt, once she'd worked out just what Father was doing, because he couldn't stand how many stupid mistakes other people made.

But now Father was the one who had made the stupid mistake. Celia knew that Father didn't care that Argent liked boys; nothing like that ever mattered to him. What he did care about was that if people *knew* that Argent liked boys, it would give the king an excuse to refuse to give him a royal princess for his wife, and maybe even to disinherit him. Father had just been trying to teach Argent not to *get caught,* and it had never occurred to him that Argent wanted love more than power.

It had thrown him completely off his stride. At first he didn't even seem to know what to do about Celia, even though that was perfectly obvious. At the breakfast table the very next morning, he said to her, remotely, "I mean to write to Grand Duke Preine today, to discuss a betrothal between you," and she stared at him out of her red-rimmed sandy eyes and said, "What?"

Father actually began delivering her a lecture that he must have had ready for many years, to quash her anticipated objections to the match, in his most cold and unyielding tones. "His Grace is lately widowed, and has no sons—"

"But I'm going to marry Gorthan now," Celia said, bewildered. It didn't make any sense to her. They didn't need to wait for another generation anymore. She was a *sorceress.* The king would instantly snatch her up for Crown Prince Gorthan, and it wouldn't offend any of the great lords of the kingdom in the slightest. She was surprised that Father hadn't already sent to tell him. "Aren't you going to write to the *king*?"

Father paused and stared at her, his cup halfway to his mouth—so did a shocked Unter and the table servants and a frozen, wide-eyed Roric, who didn't even know what had happened with Argent last night, and had been hunching over his plate and shoveling in food in his usual way—and then Father put down his cup, his face rigid, and said very shortly, "Yes. You're right," and got up at once to go and send the letter to the king, and Celia only then realized how badly off he was.

She was badly off herself, too, but she hadn't made a stupid mistake, at least. She'd made a *horrible* one, but that wasn't the same thing at all. And she wasn't sorry to be marrying Crown Prince Gorthan instead of Grand Duke Preine, even if she didn't for an instant believe any of the spun-sugar tales of how handsome and clever and brave the prince was; she'd only ever learn anything about him once she'd actually met him. But at least he *wasn't* a cowardly old man of forty-five who'd avoided ever fighting in the summer war with an excuse of bad knees, and who always fell asleep directly after eating too much dinner, the handful of times he'd come to visit, and snored.

Celia even ended up having to tell Roric about Argent herself, and that he was now the heir of their house, because three days passed and Father still hadn't done it.

And then Roric only stared at her and said, "I don't believe you."

"I'm not lying," Celia had said coldly.

Roric was silent, working it through, and then said, "Argent's *gone*? He just—*left*?" Celia was half ready to stab him with a dagger, or curse *him*, as soon as he fully grasped it and she had to watch the glow of gloating joy rising through him, but instead Roric just got up and went away, his narrow weaselly face gone blank, and later that day, he came to speak to her in her chambers and said flatly, "No one's ever cared about me. Not Father, not you, not even the servants. Argent's the only one you cared about."

"Yes," Celia said, because that was true. *She* wasn't going to be a liar, and pretend otherwise. She didn't care about Roric, but he was still her brother. He deserved that much honesty from her—that least little thing that Argent had refused to give her.

"And now he's gone away and left us," Roric said. "But Father still doesn't care. He won't even look at me at table. I'm his heir now, and I had to find out from you." He swallowed, the lump moving visibly in his skinny throat. "He didn't even put me in the register of nobility when I was born. He only wanted me to be *useful* for Argent."

"For Argent and me," Celia agreed. That was true also.

Roric nodded. "Well, I wasn't going to be," he said. "I

had to pretend I didn't mind, because I couldn't do anything about it yet, but I knew I wasn't going to be useful for anyone who didn't care about me at all. Who wasn't going to do anything for *me*."

Celia blinked. It didn't make her angry; that seemed fair enough. It just hadn't ever before occurred to her to wonder what Roric was thinking, or what he wanted. "Why are you telling me now?" she asked. It didn't seem like a very good idea. If she went and told Father that Roric meant to be troublesome, he'd probably go and get himself a fourth wife, and try to have another son.

"Because caring about people who don't care back is stupid, and you're not," Roric said. "You were just little. You didn't know you were being stupid. That's why you cared about Argent, even though he didn't care about you."

"He did!" she snapped.

"Not enough," Roric said, and that was unarguably true, even if it made her throat swell and her eyes sting. Then Roric took a deep breath and said baldly, "*Would* you care?"

"What?" Celia said, too wretched to work out what he meant.

"Father won't," Roric said. "I know he won't. I could become a great knight or the king myself and he still wouldn't care. But I thought you might, now that you know you were being stupid about Argent. Because if you'd care—then I'd care, too. Then we'd have each other, at least. And maybe I'm not Argent, but I know it's better to care."

She stared at him, and then blurted, "*How* do you know?" almost angrily. She knew he was right, even with the sharp bitter ache in her chest, or maybe because of it, but she didn't know how Roric knew.

"Because she cared," Roric said. "Your mother. She had the nurse bring me to sit with her every day. I was little, but she let me wind her thread, even if I dropped the bobbins, and pluck her lute strings. She gave me tea. And when we knew you were coming, I cried, because I thought she wouldn't want me anymore, and she told me you'd be my sib, and love me, and asked me to promise to love you back. But I couldn't, after you killed her," he added. "I didn't want to love you. And you didn't want to love me, either. But—I did promise her. So now I will, if you will," he finished, defiantly, and halfway daring her to say *no*.

Celia wanted to say no. The place where Argent had been in her heart was still raw and burning-sore, and thinking of putting Roric in it instead felt like replacing silver with dross. She wasn't even sure that she *could*. She looked at Roric, thin and lank-haired and spotty, his teeth crooked and his shoulders stooped, awkward and not very clever and not very kind, and she couldn't imagine it.

But she'd never known her mother. The only thing Father had ever told her was that she was a daughter of the royal house, descended of sorcery, and the only thing Argent had ever told her, vaguely, was that she'd been beautiful and nice. And now it seemed that her mother had tried to give Roric to her. She'd wanted her child to love Roric, and for him to love her. She'd *cared*.

"All right," Celia said. "Yes. I'll care, if you'll care," and she stood up and put her hand out, and he put his out, and they shook on the bargain.

CELIA STILL WASN'T SURE HOW to *do* it, but she thought about what Roric had told her, and then she went and found Unter and said, "What was my mother's favorite winter sitting room?"

Unter knew, of course, and in an hour he had it opened up for her. It was a round southeast tower room with three windows, each with a narrow border made of enchanted summerglass that made the light coming into the room brilliant and golden, even though the day outside was pale grey with a fine drizzle coming down, as days often were at Castle Todholme during the autumn and the winter. Celia stood looking out at the shifting light of the clouds and the shadowy mountains when they peeked out of the mist, while the servants brought in furnishings gathered back from the rooms they'd drifted to over the years: two tapestries of silk and wool with a single red-capped song-spinner on each one, made to face one another and frame the doorway with lute and fife; three low-backed wide seats of gilt wood with velvet cushions that fit just beneath each window, and a few padded stools for other seats to fill out the room. A screen of wrought iron to stand before the fireplace, and a soft woolen rug to go over the wooden floor; a few chests to hold shawls and blankets; a few small tables and one large one of inlaid wood and bone.

When everything else was done, Celia herself went to her rooms and brought back the beautiful tea service that Father had ordered taken out of storage and given to her on her tenth birthday: the magical teapot, of summer make, in the shape of a bird with its wings outspread and its beak open to sing the tea out, always hot, and the cups like nests with branches to hold them by.

She arranged it carefully on the large table, and then told Unter, "Please ask my brother if he'd like to come and sit with me to do his work." Unter only stared at her blankly, and then she added, "Roric," pointedly, and he twitched and said, "Of course, my lady."

Roric came, with his box of figuring. Father *had* arranged for him to have excellent tutors from early on, and they were drilling the keeping of accounts into him, even though he hadn't any gift for numbers. If he didn't finish all his exercises, he was punished, so he was always carrying the lap desk with his papers in it everywhere, when he wasn't bent over it in some corner, scratching away with pen and ink and squinting. He stopped on the threshold of the room and looked at Celia, and she said, "Come sit by the windows. The light's good here," and poured him a cup of tea, into one of the bird-nest cups.

He sat down slowly on the second bench beside her and held the cup between his hands as if it were full of baby birds he was trying to save. She'd opened one window to the breath of autumn air coming in, the cool rainy breeze, but the room was small and the fire kept it cozy, the colors of the rug and the tapestries bright in the summerglass glow, a jewel-box for them to sit in, as if they were both the jewels of their house. Roric looked around, and his mouth trembled, and to stop it he bent his head and sipped the tea in silence until it was all gone.

The next morning, when he came to join her again, he brought a large silk bag, creased and crumpled as if it had been crammed in somewhere hidden away, and silently thrust it at her. She opened it up and found it full of fine embroidery threads of wool and silk, and in another pouch, carefully folded up, a beautiful long panel of embroidery, meant to go around the bottom of a skirt when it was done. A scene of the Summer Lands with knights in silver and gold chasing one another with their swords, with a red-capped song-spinner playing and a princess looking out over them from a tower made of grey stones;

a shaihul with its wingscales done in iridescent purples rearing up against a dragon in red-gold, and at the end, over the Green Bridge, a grove of trees that was barely half grown in thread: the trunks just hollow outlines in pale birch white, with only a few green leaves upon the branches.

Celia held it across her hands, and touched it with the tips of her fingers. She hadn't ever been an especially brilliant needlewoman; she had always just done embroidery while she watched Argent training, to have a thing to do which Father would approve of enough not to speak ominously of idle hands. But she knew she'd take care, she'd keep the fabric properly taut and make every stitch just right, to finish this piece for her wedding.

"I took her lute, too," Roric said, a little belligerently. "But they found that and took it away from me. Father didn't want me to have it."

Celia understood why Father had done that, too. Roric's mother had been a tavern musician; for Roric to play would remind others too much about the lowly match, and his own low birth, and Father had wanted the realm to forget about that, so the lords wouldn't mind his heirs making royal matches.

"I'll ask Unter to find it for me," she said.

From then on, they spent most of their days together. The lute was sour, but Celia got Unter to get a musician from the town to come and show them how to tune it, and how to play. She pretended the lessons were for her, and not Roric, but she didn't really need to bother. Father didn't even notice. These days he was spending most of his time sitting alone in his study, without a lamp, staring at a low fire and neglecting his affairs.

Roric worked on his figuring, and Celia had a stack of books to read, in the good light—the famous one that Witch-Queen Selina's chief councillor Bertram had written about her and her Seven Wyrds, after her death, and others about the more-misty stories of the sorceresses of old before her.

The greater the Wyrd a sorceress evokes, the greater the power it raises, Councillor Bertram's book explained, in what she'd once thought were dry and boring terms. *The power thus raised will remain at her command, until spent in some working of her will, the which if it be a great action upon the world will consume a large portion of that power, and if a small one but a little, the rest remaining ready to her hand, until by many such acts she has made use of it all. Then being so worn out, the supply shall not be renewed save by the evocation of another Wyrd, which cannot be done merely at will; this much Her Majesty told me, when once I asked her, and though she would speak no more of how her own Wyrds came, we may well understand, by those receipts of her days which I have herein recounted, and those tales we have of the sorceresses of older times, that a Wyrd comes only through a great wringing-out of the heart and mind.*

The words now seemed painfully true to Celia: her

heart had been wrung mercilessly, and magic had come squeezing out of it, in a gush of wrath and blood and sorrow. She hadn't done much more sorcery since, except to light five candles and put them out again, held in the hands of five witnesses of good character and true birth called up from the town by lots, to prove that the power was there. She didn't need to prove it to herself. She could feel it moving through her, like a current flowing hidden beneath the surface of a river, either cold or hot, sometimes quicker and sometimes dragging. And she didn't want to use any of it up if she didn't have to. She was sure that she'd need almost all of it to undo even part of her curse.

She'd sent messengers riding after Argent, and to the Green Bridge, but so far no one had caught him. She had no idea how to mend the curse she'd made, or at least to find some way around it, but she had to try. She was only grateful that she hadn't done anything that would be impossible to undo; she was glad that she hadn't wished Argent a heart of glass, or told him to go jump off a mountain. But that was a cold comfort. She knew it was almost the worst thing she could have done to him, because he'd thrown away everything else. He'd given up his name and home and family, his power in the world and the pride and fame he'd won with his years of hard work and drill, all to be free to go and find someone to fall in love with, who'd love him back.

She had to fix it, even if Argent hadn't loved *her*—even if she was still angry and wounded deep in her own heart. But to her surprise and almost her sorrow, it had already become easier to forgive him. The last small hot flame of rage was dying away inside her a little more with every day spent in the cool peace of her mother's room, with Roric sitting next to her, *wanting* to be next to her: someone for her to love, who meant to love her back, as if she'd stolen Argent's dream and kept it for herself.

She'd discovered that she could be *useful* herself, to Roric. When they were eating alone together, she told him bluntly that he needed to improve his table manners, and to bathe more often and take better care of his teeth. He'd been neglected after her birth, the nurse abandoning him in a hurry to take care of the more-valued newborn child, and the servants had only indifferently looked after him, so no one had taught him how he *should* be looked after, even by himself.

At first Roric scowled at her about the reminders, and snapped, "I know!" when it was plain that he didn't, and stormed off; she was annoyed enough to almost stop wanting to sit with him. But at breakfast the next morning, he'd washed his face and cleaned his teeth properly, and he watched her as she ate and carefully mimicked her manners. He came back to the sitting room that day pretending they hadn't quarreled at all, but she didn't mind;

she preferred the apology he'd already made, by listening to her.

When he lost his temper one day struggling through a page of accounts that wouldn't add up properly, and started scratching over the whole page back and forth with his pen, she caught his hand to stop him before he ruined it badly enough to be punished. "It's stupid!" he said, furious and miserable. "It doesn't make any sense!"

So she made up a story for him out of the numbers, about a troop of summer knights being defeated by spring lambs throwing horseshoes over a wall built out of sacks of flour. It didn't make sense either, but at least he laughed, and then looked surprised at the sound out of his own mouth, and was able to work through the page from the beginning.

Even in just a few weeks, Roric was already looking better, *happier*. They told more account-stories to each other together, one step at a time as he came to each new number in the ledger, and the work of it stopped being a burden to him. He liked to make up rhymes, and sometimes he even sang them out loud—more often after he stopped looking guiltily at the door, afraid of being overheard and caught. And Celia understood, seeing the change in him, that it made her *matter* to him. She wasn't just a doll that he was playing with that he could put down carelessly and never really miss, like she had been to Argent.

That thought still stung, but not terribly, even though Argent had only been gone for so short a time. It was already much worse to worry about *him*, and whether he'd already vanished into the Summer Lands forever, doomed to live all his days without love. "I don't want to stop caring about Argent," she said, when Roric, jealous, tried to say she shouldn't be upset. "It wasn't all stupid. He did care about me, even if I cared more," which now she could believe, with the sharp agony fading. "And it wasn't *his* fault that Father doesn't care about you," she added.

Roric scowled at that, too, but then he spent the next two days bent over the big household ledger, and at the end of it he told her abruptly that they could afford to offer a purse of fifty silver coins for any song-spinner who came out of the Summer Lands and brought them a true story about Argent.

"Grand Duke Torvald offers thirty gold for the best summerling songs, and he usually gets at least ten each year," Roric said, a little sullenly, as she stared at him. "We'll hear whatever there is to hear, at least," and Celia realized that he'd made himself *useful* to Argent, for her sake. She put down her embroidery and got up and went to him and kissed his cheek and hugged his thin shoulders while he flushed and stared at the ground trying not to show how much he liked it.

A few days later, though, she had to start worrying about herself, instead. The king's reply to Father's letter came as quick as a messenger could have ridden to the capital and back. He told Father that he wanted Celia for the prince, which was only to be expected, and that he wanted her sent to the capital so she could be married right away, which wasn't to be expected at all, when she was only twelve and barely become a woman. Celia was taken aback; it wasn't a reasonable thing to ask. Even a proxy marriage would have been a little strange. She wasn't some foreign princess, with her marriage the seal on an important treaty.

"He wants you under his control as soon as possible," Father said, dismissively, and wrote back to say he couldn't agree to have her married until she was eighteen, although they were honored by the betrothal.

Celia wasn't sure she believed that comforting explanation. If that was what the king had been thinking, surely he'd recognize that Father was going to keep her under *his* control for as long as he could possibly justify, and there wasn't any point asking. But she also couldn't think of any other good reasons why the king would want to get her so young, which only left unpleasant ones. But she couldn't get Father to put his own brain on the problem. He was still refusing to care about anything, since what he'd cared about the most was gone.

"You could use your magic," Roric said, but Celia couldn't see what to *do* with the magic. She could have smashed open a castle gate or blasted a dozen enemies into smoldering ash. She could have called down a hurricane or raised a flood. She could have raised the dead or cured the sick. Selina had done all those things, and when Celia read about them, she felt the magic still churning inside her, eager to answer, and could see just how she'd do it herself.

Or she could have marched into the capital and taken control of the mind of the king and forced him to tell her. But then she might as well simply crown herself the new Witch-Queen, and just accept that the rest of her life would be spent watching her back for assassins and her front for liars and cheats. Celia didn't want that any more than Father had wanted it, back when he could have taken the throne himself. She'd been perfectly ready to marry Prince Gorthan, with Father and sorcery on her side to make it an equal match, and to work with him to make a happy and well-run kingdom, and a happy and well-run life for both of them inside it. She'd even let herself imagine, before the ominous message had come, that maybe she could *care* about him, and he about her; she'd thought that she would ask him to, when they met, the way Roric had asked her, and see what he said. Now she was just afraid, and she didn't even know what she was afraid of.

Roric did hire a passing song-spinner to quietly go to the capital and dig up anything he could about Gorthan, but when the spinner came back, all he could tell them was that Gorthan had a reputation for courtesy and caution. He'd had a couple of common-born mistresses, pretty girls within a year or two of his own age, who had been very happy in their positions as far as anyone knew, and he'd ended the liaisons and arranged marriages for them with landed knights after they'd each borne him a bastard child. Neither of the children had lived past the age of two, but that was still a sensible thing for a prince to do, to avoid having one woman bearing him many children, and setting her up as a rival to a future queen.

He sounded as good as you could hope for, when you were marrying a throne, and a little uneasily Celia tried to believe that Father was right, and that the king had just thought it was worth a try to get her. Maybe he'd hoped that Father would want to get the match sewn up, and become the father-in-law of the crown prince right away. But she couldn't quite convince herself.

After the song-spinner left them, no better off for his information, and she was sitting silently, Roric said abruptly, "We need to take over the estates." When she looked at him in surprise, he said, "Father's not doing any work anymore. I can see the accounts are getting into a mess. For now everyone's still doing their work and paying their taxes, because they're used to him watching, but soon they'll notice that he isn't. Then everything will start to fall apart, and the king will find out, and he won't be afraid of Father anymore. We need to keep his reputation strong, and make sure we still have men and money, if we need them. That's all we can do for now, so we should do it. You can always kill them all with sorcery if you have to," he added.

It was good advice. Celia nodded.

CELIA TOLD UNTER TO BRING things to them if Father didn't do anything about them for a week, and he started bringing them almost everything. Anything that Father would have done in person before, Roric went out and did himself, taking Unter along, pretending that he was being trained to run the estates and Father was having him observed every step of the way. "Give bad orders once in a while, too," Celia told him, "and then go back the next day and change it, acting sullen, as if Father's overridden you." Roric nodded.

Celia also wrote letters to every high-ranking noblewoman in the kingdom who didn't have a daughter or niece of her own to resent Gorthan passing over, and humbly told them that her mother had spoken of them as wise and kind, and asked them for their advice to a motherless girl who was being advanced to a station beyond anything she'd expected. She got many replies, full of reams of bad and often contradictory advice—sometimes within the same letter—and to each one sent back effusive thanks and promises to follow the advice to the letter, and the small gift of a fine silk lace triangle embroidered by her own hand, the sort to be kept tucked into the top of a corset and unseen by others.

The Dowager Marchioness of Travinia, who lived at court and according to the song-spinners had a reputation as a poisonous harpy, wrote, *Oh, I think you'll do well enough on your own, little vixen, even if you do marry at sixteen. Save me a good seat at the coronation; I'm an old woman and my sight isn't what it used to be.*

Celia wrote back, *My father would be honored to be your escort,* to thank her for the warning, slipped subtly into the letter: so the king didn't mean to wait past sixteen, and the marchioness didn't approve. Celia didn't much want to be married at sixteen herself, especially when Gorthan was so much older than her, but all in all she felt comforted. That *did* make some sense of the king asking for her at twelve, if he'd done it meaning to seem more reasonable when he demanded her at sixteen, so he could get her at least a year or two sooner than Father might have wanted to hand her over.

She also got a letter from Gorthan himself. It was too formal to tell her much about him, except that he *was* cautious, but at least there wasn't anything awful in it, and there wasn't anything suspiciously wonderful in it, either. He just wrote that he and his father rejoiced with all Prosper that the gift of sorcery had flowered once again, surely

the reward of her father's courage and service to the kingdom. He thanked her for being willing to trust him with
her hand, and hoped she continued in good health and
humor until they met, which would be a day of great hap-
piness for him and the whole kingdom.

She did use a little sorcery on the letter, enough to be
sure that there wasn't an outright lie in it. Of course all
sorts of awful possibilities could still be lurking beneath
those polite and careful words, but at least Gorthan wasn't
more resentful than glad about sorcery appearing in her
father's line, which she'd worried he would be, and he
wasn't wishing for her untimely death. It eased her mind.
If nothing else, it really did make too much sense for the
king and Gorthan to want her to bear him a child. They
almost couldn't want anything else.

The months slipped by quickly with the work that was
now theirs. She turned thirteen in the spring, and a few
weeks later, summer rolled back over Prosper like a golden
wave. The Green Bridge appeared out of the river mists
and the summer games began, and almost at once, song-
spinners began to arrive at Castle Todholme to collect
purses of silver for one story after another about the
Knight of the Woven Blade, questing through the Summer Lands, none of which made Celia feel any better.
They were all true, she could feel their truth even without
using magic to check, and every single one was about
nothing but elaborate heroics. Sir Argent had defeated a

giant, three ettins, a pack of trolls; he'd rescued three different summerling ladies from terrible menaces; he'd
climbed the Golden Mountain and defeated the serpent
guardian to bring a cupful of water from the spring back
to save an ailing summer lord who'd been poisoned by a
lady that he'd spurned.

"Did Argent stay there?" Celia asked, unhappily, already knowing the answer even before the song-spinner
said that he'd stayed only one more night at the summer
lord's castle before traveling on. Summer stories had a
rhythm and a pattern to them, and she knew in her belly
exactly how that one *should* have ended: with the summer
lord rising healed and radiant from his bed to catch the
hand of the heroic knight who had saved him, and asking
him to stay forever as his honored guest. Her curse had
broken the story: Argent's story that should have been.

She tried again to send word to him, but no song-
spinner managed to find him. The summer ended and the
mists closed around the Green Bridge once more. A whole
year gone, since Argent had left, and Celia wept the morning when she heard the autumn walls going up. In the sitting room that day, Roric gave her a blank sheet out of his
papers, and she marked out all the weeks until the next
summer, and crossed them off one after another as the
year rolled past. The accounts and estate business came
endlessly, but Celia and Roric told their way through them
with more stories, and sometimes now Roric played the

lute along. On her fourteenth birthday she received another letter from Prince Gorthan, almost exactly the same as the first, with wishes for her health.

The next summer brought even more of the dreadful, grand stories, so many of them that Roric had to lower the prize money, and soon they didn't even have to pay any at all. Songs about the legendary Knight of the Woven Blade were sweeping around the kingdom and coming to Castle Todholme without any encouragement at all. Listening to them, full of the ever-greater and ever-wilder heroics Argent kept performing, Celia felt sick to her stomach with tears; she was back on the library balcony, listening to what Father had done to Argent, only *she* had done it. She had told Argent what he couldn't have, and left him with only the sword to love, chasing after a hollow glory he didn't want.

The last of her own resentment was long gone; by now it was only a distant memory of something stupid and childish she'd felt, that had made her do something horrible to her brother, which she regretted desperately. "I have to go," she said, low, at the end of that summer, watching the autumn wind blowing the rain into streaks like tears across the window of their sitting room. "It's never going to work, sending a trader to find him. I'll have to go to the Summer Lands myself. Next summer," she added. "Before I'm married."

She expected Roric to tell her not to be stupid. It *was*

stupid for her to go to the Summer Lands. She was the daughter of Veris the Fox—an honored enemy, but the summerlings' worst enemy all the same. And aside from that, they would be fools not to see that a sorceress made Prosper dangerously strong, maybe even strong enough to invade *them*, in turn. The summerlings had magic of their own, but their magic was all in beauty and craft—fine delicate tools next to the sledgehammer of sorcery.

And even if the summerlings didn't do a thing to her, she could easily get lost or hurt all on her own. Traveling alone in the Summer Lands was dangerous even for trained knights and experienced song-spinners, who were welcome guests. She'd never traveled more than a month away from Castle Todholme, and then it had been with Father and a large escort of servants and guards. She didn't even like hunting or riding or long walks. Chances were that she'd fall into a corpse-flower maw or stumble over an archodile or just start walking around in circles without realizing and die long before she ever found Argent.

But instead Roric was silent, and then he said, "I'll go with you." She looked at him surprised. Argent hadn't earned that from him. Argent really *hadn't* cared about Roric at all, even to play with him like a doll, or give him the least bit of attention. And she knew that Roric was still resentful; he'd been running the estates for two years by then, with only her to help him, and Father still hadn't formally named him the heir, or done anything to acknowledge his work at all. But Roric said, "You can't do it alone. I'll go with you, and we'll try."

THEY SPENT THE REST OF the autumn and the winter practicing, going on walks together through the mountains and hills around Todholme. Roric practiced the lute even more, and Celia read many books about the Summer Lands—accounts from song-spinners who'd been and come back again—and made a list of what was important to take and how to pack it, so the two of them could carry it all by themselves without the help of servants. But they didn't get the chance. In the spring, right after Celia turned fifteen, another letter came, but this wasn't from Gorthan. The king had sent Father a royal command to bring her to the Green Bridge, to be married in the old royal palace that stood near the border of the Summer Lands, at the great festival that would open the summer tourneys.

There wasn't any good way to refuse. It was a formal command, with the words *without fail,* and also a little too reasonable. King Morthimer had written that it was past time for Prince Gorthan to be married, and everyone in the kingdom would agree with that. He was nine-and-twenty, and he still didn't have even a bastard child living.

And more people than not would even agree with the king that fifteen was old enough for her to be married, since she wouldn't bear her first child before sixteen.

Just barely reasonable, and nothing in the letter was a *lie*, but Celia was certain that it also wasn't the real reason. The king had wanted her at twelve, and the prince couldn't possibly have gotten an heir on her then without shocking the country and risking her life, so that wasn't what he really wanted. It was only the excuse that the king was using now to make Father hand her over to him as quickly as possible. And he wanted that *too* much; making it an ultimatum was a risk, because there were also plenty of people who would agree with *Father*, if he dug in his heels and refused to hand over his daughter so young, and then the king would have to decide between giving in and looking weak, or declaring Father a traitor and picking a fight with him, which would have made him look unreasonable enough to let Celia just take the throne with sorcery after all, with most people, especially the common folk, ready to take their part.

Father did finally recognize that something was wrong, but he'd spent too much time with his brain shut up inside a dark room, and he couldn't take it out and use it again right away. He said finally, "I'll muster a thousand men for our escort, and raise another seven thousand, in case it comes to war," but that was just flailing. He didn't really know what to do. He'd still know what to do if it did come to fighting, but Celia didn't believe it would. The king wouldn't count on winning a war against Father—no one would have—so it couldn't be fighting.

"I'm coming too," Roric said, as they left his study together.

"You can't," Celia said. "If they killed Father *and* you, they could do anything they wanted with me, and there wouldn't even be anyone to object. I can't just slaughter the entire army of Prosper."

"If they kill Father, they can do anything they want with you anyway," Roric said, which was probably true. "Anyway, I won't let anyone *know* I'm coming. I'll dress like a song-spinner and go to the Green Bridge as if I'm thinking of going into the Summer Lands for the season. No one in the royal court knows anything about me. They might not even know I exist."

Roric left the castle that same day, with her mother's lute and a red cap on his head. While the more elaborate preparations for her own journey were made, Celia grimly finished the last part of the embroidery, a little bit quicker than she'd meant to, so the two figures being married under the trees had to be left a bit indistinct, and she sewed it onto a beautiful silk gown of green and yellow, the colors of summer, for her wedding day.

Castle Todholme was a long way from the border: Father hadn't wanted to be in range of a surprise attack. It took two weeks to make the journey to the Green Bridge.

She sat tensely next to Father in the coach the whole way, and it wasn't reassuring to feel him just as taut beside her. On the last night of the journey, he ordered his men to stop and make camp a little early, at the crest of a hill overlooking the Evergreen Valley. He and Celia got out of the coach; she followed him to the ridge and they looked down together into the wide green half valley below, with the snaking line of the Meanwhile River running along the border of the Summer Lands, still shrouded in thick mist: it wasn't yet the first day of summer. The Green Bridge wasn't really there yet, but you could glimpse it like a shadow, on the verge of emerging from the mist.

Taverns and market stalls were clustered on either side of the royal road running from the Green Bridge. Celia had heard many of their song-spinner guests talk with enthusiasm about the reopening of the Summer Market, and all the lovely enchanted summer work they'd seen. But there were many more half-crumbled stalls still abandoned than there were repaired, and all of them looked deserted at the moment, as if the mortal tradesmen were hanging back and would only turn up after the summerlings arrived.

The challenge grounds were just a large rectangle mowed into the ground near the river, with pavilions set up around it and one block of tall wooden stands. It wasn't especially impressive. Their training yard at Castle Todholme was almost as big. The old royal palace stood on the other side of the road, upon the tallest rise along the bank of the river, but it was more than half a ruin, of pale soft limestone streaked with dirt. For a hundred years of war, no one had lived there, and no one seemed to have done much work to rebuild it since. Prince Gorthan wasn't even staying inside. The royal flag with its crown was flying from a large pavilion outside the walls, surrounded by a large company of royal armsmen, who looked more like a military camp than an embassy, with many sentries on high alert.

Father stood silently frowning down into the valley while the leading edge of nightfall gradually crept in from the east. "What is it?" Celia said, looking at him.

"*This* is what's wrong," he said after a moment, like rusty gears turning. "It's the peace that's a lie."

And as soon as he said it, Celia could see the lie of it herself. The legends all said that the town of Green Bridge was almost part of the Summer Lands, truly halfway between. The trees never lost their leaves, and summerlings would often pole out of the river mists on an unseasonably warm day, even if the bridge wasn't open, and attend feasts in the royal palace. That was why Princess Eislaing had been able to marry Sherdan, and come to live with him here.

But the town below was just a perfectly ordinary mortal place. Some of the market stalls were nicely fixed up, others half built. There were untidy piles in places and ugly ruins left uncovered, weedy plants and irregular patches of tall grass growing. Those makeshift grounds weren't a place for the flower of summer knights to do battle. The palace ruins were picturesque but not achingly beautiful, and the towers were surrounded by the rotting heaps of the long-collapsed autumn halls, which no one had cleaned up. The summerlings hadn't really come back. They were just pretending.

"But—the summer war ended before I was born," she said. "It's been almost twenty years."

"What's twenty years to a summerling?" Father said. "They don't change. Time is a river; it carries us along. But they're only on the banks, watching it go by. They can *be* changed, if we throw a rock and hit them, but they don't change on their own." He shook his head. "If the king had let me kill Elithyon, that might have ended the war. Some other summer lord would have become king, and likely he'd have forgotten that any Elithyon and Eislaing even existed. No summer king really remembers that there was ever a king before him. But Elithyon would never give up vengeance for his sister. To him, we're still the same people who murdered her the day before yesterday. When he agreed to peace, he lied."

"But what about *our* king?" Celia said uneasily. "What's *he* lying about?"

Father was silent a long moment, and then he gave an impatient shrug. "Unless Morthimer is a complete fool, he wants you to bear Gorthan an heir. That's even more true if he knows the peace is false. And then—" He seesawed his hand. "He'll see how biddable you are. If you're difficult, or too much under my thumb, you could die in childbirth, or of some sickness."

And that all made perfect sense, only Celia felt too much that she was working on a puzzle with some pieces shoved into the wrong places, not quite fitting, and the picture not coming clear. But there still wasn't a better choice than going forward. If the summerlings were just waiting to attack again, starting a civil war in Prosper would be a terrible idea, especially on the first day of summer.

They rode down early the next morning, and even as they came, the mist was rolling back from a shining bridge of living wood, vines full of leaves and opening into flowers. Celia couldn't help but put her head out of the carriage window to watch it stretching out for the bank. Even though nothing about the town had changed, Celia was glad she'd seen it from a distance, the day before, to recognize the lie: all the disrepair she'd seen was hard to notice with the warm fragrant summer breeze coming down the road, and flowers blooming on either side.

Father encamped their men in a solid block just north of the tourney grounds, near a stand of trees he'd marked out the evening before, which he knew were real; he put a small company of two dozen men hidden there, with three fast horses apiece, and had them lay a ring of salt around their camp. "If something goes wrong, we'll go straight there, and run for the mountains," he said. But Celia was sure that nothing was going to go wrong with that much warning. "Don't use sorcery until you have to," he added. "It's a blunt instrument. If you have to use it against them at all, likely the only sensible thing you can do is kill them." It was a warning she didn't need, and which wasn't comforting when sorcery was the only power she had to defend herself.

A royal messenger arrived while they were still putting up tents, and told Father that the wedding would be held that very evening before the opening feast began. He pointed out a small beautiful grove that Celia hadn't noticed before, on the riverbank near the palace: a stand of golden-barked trees hung with swaths of green silk and white flowering vines. There was an enormous white pavilion up on the other side of it, full of feasting tables, with servants already bustling around them to lay down the trenchers and dress them with flowers. "Prince Gorthan sends his greetings and best wishes, Your Grace, and thanks you for the honor of entrusting him with your daughter. He will come to you at sunset, to escort her ladyship to the wedding grove, where she and the prince will pledge their troth," the messenger said.

He wasn't lying, and more than that, he seemed sincerely excited, and eyed her with the avid curiosity of a man who thought he was looking at his future queen. At least *he* thought the wedding was going to happen. After he left, with many bows and smiles in her direction, she said to Father, "Maybe it's *you* they're going to murder," which would have made some sense, if the king didn't realize that the summerlings were going to break the peace. Once she was married to Gorthan, he could get rid of Father, and have a young sorceress completely in his power.

Father put on his armor, and kept all his men on high alert, but no one attacked them. As the sun was going down, a company detached itself from the royal camp and came towards their own, but it was only an honor guard of two dozen knights in full plate, with cloaks of royal blue, and in their midst a tall man, not quite young anymore, with a serious face and a trimmed brown beard, in beautifully engraved steel armor and a cloak of purple, who was soon bowing over her hand: Gorthan.

"Your Highness," she said, making her curtsy, and then lifted her eyes and looked him anxiously in the face.

He looked down at her soberly, without any false pretense at enthusiasm, and said, "I'm glad to meet you, my lady. Let us go to the wedding-grove," and held his hand out for hers. She looked at Father; he just gave a small jerk of his chin: *go on.* She put her hand into Gorthan's. It was hard in a familiar way, like Father's and like Argent's: a swordsman's hand, with calluses from drill. The royal guard closed ranks around them, and her own honor guard of ten men fell in at their heels, Father and his own guard behind them, and they walked together towards the beautiful grove, trailing a small army of soldiers and mutual distrust behind them.

Celia was still uneasy, but she couldn't help but think how silly it was to be married this way. She looked over at Gorthan, and when he looked back at her she said, trying to share the joke, "We should have brought a drummer, to keep the time," and he darted a look back at the marching pack of men and gave a small involuntary snort of laughter. For a moment his face had good humor in it, a sparkle. He quenched it back to seriousness a moment later, but she felt a little burst of hope. Surely someone who could laugh at himself a little bit couldn't be so terrible to be married to.

They came to the grove, and a pale and nervous priest was waiting by the front of it. He said to her anxiously, "My lady, I ask you to aver that you come here with your family's consent and of your own free will to be married to the prince, as your king has commanded, and go hence with him to his home," darting a look at Gorthan, as if he wasn't sure what he'd do if she said no.

"I do aver it," Celia said, and Gorthan heaved a deep breath and led her past the priest and into the grove. They had to lift aside a curtain of the flowering vines to go inside, and a delicate wafting of perfume came off them that tugged up a fragment of memory of something she'd never known, just barely familiar in some strange way and already slipping away. She tried to catch it, and for a moment in her mind's eye she had a bright and vivid glimpse of her sitting room back in Castle Todholme, with a woman she didn't know sitting inside it, working on a band of embroidery, and Celia caught the faint scent of her skin.

Her eyes were prickling with tears, a sensation beautiful and painful at the same time. Then Gorthan's hand was drawing her forward through the trees, and another curtain of flowering vines brought another scrap of memory: sitting crying with her knee bloodied in the garden and her nurse fluttering anxious, and then Argent bending down to her, smiling, picking her up. He was saying something to her, but the words were lost, and didn't matter; her head was nestling down on his shoulder, and his arms were strong around her, safe.

She had to put her hand out to stop a vine coming into her face, and suddenly she was swallowing laughter instead: sitting in the tower herself with Roric, telling him another one of the silly account-stories she made up for him, each one a ridiculous summer battle, only this one was all the best parts out of all the stories, somehow woven up together into the funniest story she'd never told, and Roric had stopped doing any of the actual figuring for laughter, and she was giggling with him even as she went on telling it.

She couldn't see her way, or any path through the trees and vines; she almost couldn't see Gorthan ahead of her at the length of her arm and his. She kept following him, feeling a little like she was in a dream, and more of one with every step, until suddenly she was alongside him and he was lifting aside a final curtain of vines to let them into a clearing that seemed bigger than the entire grove had been, and all around on every side nothing but solid walls of trees. And in the middle of the grove waiting for them stood a man, only it wasn't a man at all. It was a summerling.

Celia had never seen a summerling before, except in pictures, and pictures weren't anything like. He was tall and impossibly beautiful, like a statue someone had worked on for a long time, his skin a burnished deep bronze and his long hair going from the same bronze at the roots to palest white-gold at the ends, and wrapped with spiraling bands of gold. His eyes were brilliant green and painted with a darker green all around. He wore a suit of golden armor with a green cape that wasn't made of cloth but of leaves, and instead of a helm he wore a crown. He fit so well into the grove that it didn't seem like a surprise to see him at first, and Celia only slowly turned her head to look at Gorthan.

He was looking straight on at the summerling, in a way that was somehow deliberately avoiding looking at her, and he said, "Hail, Elithyon. This is Celia, descended of Selina and of Sherdan the Betrayer, and she has come of her own free will to be married to you, as my father promised, when next a sorceress was born in his line."

"No, I haven't," Celia said. "I came to be married to *you*."

But it was like speaking in a dream, trying to tell the other dream-people in it that something was wrong; neither Gorthan nor Elithyon paid any attention to her, and she couldn't seem to even try to pull her hand away. Even as she spoke, she was walking along with Gorthan towards the Summer Prince, and then she was in front of him, and she just watched him taking her hand from Gorthan as easily as if she'd given it to him.

"*No*," she said again, protesting.

"Your pledge was given before the sacred grove before you entered; too late now to try and draw it back," Elithyon said, his eyes on her with a poisonous gleam, and she realized too late how careful they'd been, the whole time, only to say *the prince*. She couldn't seem to do anything—she couldn't seem to *decide* to do anything—as Elithyon lifted up her hand. And with his own hand gloved in thick leather and shining golden mail and scales of gold, he put a thin ring of coal-dark metal onto her finger that burned as he slid it on, and she jerked back out of the dream in a gasp, cold water thrown in her face. It seemed suddenly ridiculous that she had just *gone along*, but when she tried to wrench her hand loose, Elithyon was holding her in a grip she couldn't break, and when she reached for her sorcery, it felt as if her fingers were scrabbling on a sheet of the same smooth metal of that ring, refusing to get a hold. She had never spent her power except on little things, but she'd gotten used to *feeling* it within her, a river that she could dip her hand into as she liked, and now instead the river was running somewhere too deep for her to reach, sunk beneath the earth.

"You gave your word," Gorthan was saying to Elithyon. "No torment, no torture—"

"The oath I gave to your father I will keep: nothing more to be done to her than was done to my own sister," Elithyon said, a savage note. "As you cherished *her*, so shall I cherish *your* treasure."

"What are you *doing*?" Celia said to Gorthan in rising desperation; he darted a sideways look over at her as if he didn't want to, something ashamed in the movement. "Just handing me and my sorcery to them? Listen to me, they haven't really made peace! The terms are just a lie, they'll start the war again—"

"These *were* the peace terms," Gorthan said stiffly, not quite meeting her eyes. "The next sorceress of Sherdan's line, a princess of Prosper, to be the wife of the Summer Prince, the way they gave Princess Eislaing to be the wife of King Sherdan. That's what Elithyon demanded, to make peace."

"Why did you *give* those terms?" Celia said. "You could just have let my father kill him! You can do it *now*! He'll do it; he did it before, without sorcery. I'll *help*— *Please!*" she added, a cry of fear, because even though she wasn't moving, Elithyon was drawing her away with him, and she couldn't stop it. The clearing was stretching around them like a thread being drawn taut. In a moment it would reach a snapping point, and she'd be *gone*. She felt with horrible certainty that the only thing keeping her here at all, in this halfway place, was Gorthan—her only tie back to the mortal world. "Please, don't let him take me! *Why?*"

Gorthan's face moved a little with guilt, and she had an instant of hope: the pulling sensation paused for a moment, as if he *could* choose to keep her here—which he could, surely. He was also a prince, the prince she'd agreed to marry, and more so than Elithyon. And he knew it, too. But then he looked away and said, each word prying her desperate fingers off him, "We know your father's a traitor. When I was born, a soothsayer told my father that a fox would snatch the line of sorcery from our house, and take my throne as well."

"He's not!" Celia said. "*I'm* not! I came to *marry* you!" but he had already let her go. The trees at the other end of the grove were sweeping towards them like a tide, and even as Gorthan said, "I'm sorry," he was vanishing out of view, and the world slipped out from under her feet. She stumbled, just one step, and she was in the Summer Lands, with the Summer Prince holding her hand, gripped hard and tight in his own mailed fist.

SHE'D BEEN PLANNING TO GO into the Summer Lands. She'd read a thousand stories, heard a thousand songs, seen a thousand pictures drawn, even though she'd felt, the more of them she'd read, that all of them were at least half wrong, as if they were darts that had only landed at the edges of the truth. But she'd learned enough to know that what you brought into the Summer Lands shaped what you found there; back home she had a carefully chosen basket packed with useful, sensible things, which she'd meant to take with her. She'd tried to imagine the journey strongly enough to make herself brave, when she went.

But she couldn't be brave now; she didn't have her sorcery, and she didn't have the help of anyone who loved her, and she was in the hands of a summerling prince who would gladly have slaughtered every living person in all of Prosper to get his revenge, and who now meant to satisfy himself by wringing it out of *her*, instead. She was terrified, and so she was walking on a narrow, root-choked trail through a dark and brooding wood, full of shadows and half-seen looming creatures peering out of them with malicious and hungry eyes. And Elithyon saw her fear and smiled, cruel and pleased, and walked slower, so she'd be in among them for longer.

But that helped her, because seeing his pleasure made her angry, and it was easier to think when she was angry than afraid. "Did King Sherdan make Eislaing walk a mile to her wedding feast?" she said, to Elithyon.

Elithyon glared down at her. "You dare to speak her name? She who should have been your golden queen?"

"And wouldn't *she* have had the right to complain?" Celia said, grateful for everything she'd gleaned out of her half-true stories. Elithyon had sworn an oath that had tied her story up to Eislaing's; anything he did to her now needed to be bound up with something that had been done to his own sister.

"For Eislaing, the paths would have made themselves smooth and short, and bloomed for joy with flowers to have her tread upon them," Elithyon said, and Celia could hear fresh agony in every word.

We're the same people who killed his sister, and it happened the day before yesterday, Father had said.

Celia couldn't remember that kind of feeling; it had slipped out of her fingers, carried away by the river of flowing time, but she knew she'd felt it, once. If she tried, she could be back in that musty stable corridor, cold and damp with the early days of autumn, strangling tears in her throat while she listened to the one person in the world she loved the most leaving her forever, and her belly full of misery and a monstrous, devouring rage.

As that terrible memory woke in her, the trees all around her shuddered back, drawing away branches that were heavy and thick with the greenery of their endless summer that had never been touched by a hint of fall. Even Elithyon stiffened, and looked at her hand, as if to make sure that the ring he'd put upon it was still there. Celia followed his eyes, and when she looked up again, there was a short path ahead leading to a wide stone courtyard before a palace with a great feasting arranged, like a mirror of the one she'd seen being prepared on the other bank of the river. But the tables here were filled with summerlings who were glaring at her, all their faces savage with shared hate.

The courtyard of the Summer Palace didn't have a hard edge; the great flagstones of creamy-brown stone dwindled into smaller rough-edged shapes like the stones of a path, which in their turn dwindled down into little chips like the pieces of a mosaic before they at last ebbed out into dirt, and seven narrow channels of running water cut across it in flowing lines, joining into small pools that moved to new places every time she looked at them.

The palace itself surrounded the courtyard on all three other sides. The buildings were only one story, raised up off the ground on platforms, and mostly stood wide open to catch every breeze, not unlike the summer porch of a castle in Prosper. But all the pillars were the trunks of living trees, and the rafters were their branches, full of their own leaves and vines and other living plants like green starbursts clinging on wherever they could; full of the soft humming song of gleambugs darting jewel-bright among the leaves, glowing in brief spangles of green and blue. The floor she could see inside was the floor of a forest, carpeted thickly in shining deep-green moss, and here and there a hanging curtain of thread-thin vines like fine mesh hung down to shield a chamber from view.

A host of servants were coming from inside, carrying platters out to the feast tables arranged in the courtyard. There were at least fifty of them, and not more than a thousand, and that was all that Celia could be sure of. She had to stumble along with Elithyon and sit at the high table next to him, when he thrust her into the chair next to his. She was afraid to eat. Summerling food was often enchanted in the stories, and it seemed to her that every plate was full of horrible writhing shapes as it was being set in front of her, even though when she looked straight down, the dishes were beautiful and appetizing. So instead she took anything that looked like bread from the table: summerlings didn't grow wheat or grind their own flour, so it would have come from Prosper instead. She slipped it into her pockets through the slits in her skirts, and hoped to eat it later, if it still looked like bread when she took it out again.

As the feasting ended, the lower tables cleared themselves away. They too were made of living vines and branches that simply unwound from one another and rolled back into the forest dark, leaving the courtyard half empty before the high table. The summerlings had been drinking only cool sweet water until then, out of cups made of wood and leaves, which never ran dry. But now servants came around with golden flagons, filling glass drinking horns with a gush of a sweet-smelling drink whose color changed like a sunrise, swirling pink and golden and pale blue, with a pale golden froth at the top, and then a second row of servants came around with smaller silver flagons, and poured a stream of strong rich midnight-blue liquor into each horn for as long as it was held out to them, and many of the summerlings laughing held theirs out for a pour that made the whole drink darken into sunset colors instead.

After everyone had been served and all the horns filled a second time, two great drums were rolled out of the woods into the courtyard, made of huge hollow tree trunks wider across than a man's height. Braces were brought out to hold them balanced on their sides, with two players climbing up onto low stands on either side to play each one, and musicians with strange two-stringed lutes played thin high melodies while the other summerlings began to clap and shout along.

Some summerlings began to come forward to take a turn dancing facing the high table, sometimes just one, or in pairs or threes moving in perfect time with one another, with long silken sleeves and skirts rippling through the air like ribbons, and their fingers leaving sparkling traces of glowing phosphorescence like gleambugs themselves, making pictures out of the trails that lingered in the air behind them. Each new dancer picked up the pattern as they moved up to the front, keeping the trails unbroken, sometimes bringing two trails together to mingle them, or using their hands like a knife to cut apart one of the light-trails into two separate curving paths instead.

Celia forgot to be afraid for a little while, caught up in the beauty and grace, the drums echoing through the ground and into her body like heavy thunderstorms in the mountains. A new dancer came forward to the front: a beautiful summerling man with dark hair and pale grey skin, wearing red silk and silver. He followed a trio, and he moved with such speed and grace that he managed to keep all six of the light-trails they left behind them going smoothly, and suddenly Elithyon got up and left her at the table to go into the courtyard with him.

There was a faint murmuring all around, and Celia suddenly felt eyes on her again. For a while the summer-

lings had forgotten to glare at her, lost in their own mer-
rymaking, but now they all looked at her with pleased little
smirks of satisfaction while Elithyon joined the other summerling in his dance, as if she was being insulted. She
wasn't sure what was the safest feeling to show them. Did
they want her to be unhappy, or angry, or offended? She
just went on watching, trying to keep her face as neutral as
she could, so they could read whatever they wanted to into
her expression.

Elithyon and the other summerling man were reaching new heights of grace, the two of them sending a dozen
light-trails flying, throwing them out into wide shimmer-
ing loops around the whole courtyard, other summerlings
reaching up to dip their own fingers into the trails, adding
more colors to go along, and then many of them began to
come into the courtyard to join the dance—a dance that
now turned into a circle around Elithyon and his partner,
with Celia left alone and outside the gathering at the deserted high table. But she didn't mind; no one was looking
at her anymore, and the dance was so dazzling, every
movement so perfectly right, that Celia fell back into that
dreamlike fascination. She didn't even realize for a little
while that she was still watching while Elithyon was *kissing*
the other man, and even as it slowly dawned on her, she
noticed that many of the summerlings were openly em-
bracing within the dance, coming together to move in
slow lush sinuous movements against one another, hands

moving into their silken garments to trail sparkling light over naked skin.

She had only ever taken a few furtive peeks into *those* summer books, in the back corner of the market where the merchants kept them in chests under their tables. She'd never quite been able to bring herself to buy them and bring them into the castle, even after Father had sunk into his torpor: less afraid of punishment than pure embarrassment. The occasional sneaked passage hadn't been nearly enough preparation. Celia couldn't find a safe place to look; she ended up staring down at the table, but she couldn't remember to keep doing it. The music would rise to a sudden heated speed, and she'd look up, and then she'd watch for a little while, just caught by the beauty of it again, and then suddenly realize what she was watching and jerk her eyes back down.

She understood now why all the summerlings had thought she ought to feel insulted, to have her husband dancing with someone else at her wedding feast, but she was only desperately relieved. She hoped Elithyon made love with a dozen summerlings to insult her some more, and then slept for a week afterwards. No one was paying any attention to her, the rest of them also dancing and making love together as if the two were nearly the same thing, changing partners now and again. She took the chance and tried surreptitiously to take the ring off her finger with both hands underneath the table, but it wouldn't so much as turn, even when she gripped it with a corner of the tablecloth.

She thought of trying to slip away, but she was too afraid of being noticed while they were all drunk and ever more wild-spirited. There were tales of summerlings hunting mortals who'd offended them and tearing apart their prey, and she was still sewn into her heavy silken wedding-gown, which had taken two dressers to put on her, with nothing but thin slippers on her feet.

So she just tried to stay small and quiet while the wanton revelry kept going, hoping they would all fall asleep, until suddenly Elithyon was coming back to his throne, breathing hard, his skin glowing with a sheen of sweat, smiling and his eyes brilliant. He dropped into his seat and held his horn out to be refilled with sunset by two summerling servants who appeared at once with the flagons of gold and silver as if it had been a rehearsed moment. He drank and then looked over at her with a puzzled and open expression, curious and easy to read: Who was she, and what was she doing there next to him?

Celia stared back at him and could *see* the memory come rolling back over him. His hand clenched on the horn unmoving, and a blank, stricken look came into his face, as if he'd just been told something dreadful, and then he hardened back into that terrible rage and glared at her as furiously as if the brief moment of delight had never happened.

"Now you know the fate that lies before you," he said, murderously. "Think not that I will forget. Though we do not cling to the faint shades of the past as you scrabbling mortals do, I swear to you that even should a thousand of your mortal years pass, still I will remember Eislaing and seek vengeance for her pain. I will *never* love you. You will wear a crown as hollow as the one your king gave her, and be queen in nothing but name. I will never come to your bed or look at you with desire, or show you the least honor. Others shall have my love, and you shall sit beside me in silence and humiliation, and know that nothing will ever win you my heart. I swear it to you by silver and by gold."

He finished in a savage, triumphant rush, and suddenly the feasting was ending, all the music and crowd ebbing away from the courtyard and vanishing away into the palace like an unstoppered bottle pouring out, and Elithyon had her hand again. Celia had to stand up or be pulled, and with a single step she was suddenly with him at the side of the courtyard and being drawn into a tower made of pale white stone that didn't fit into the rest of the palace at all. It looked just like the winter tower of a mortal castle, eight-sided with the hinge sockets waiting for autumn walls to be put in, and when he pulled her inside, the floor of the tower was even tiled, with the ventilation holes in the back corner to let the smoke out of the oven that would warm them from beneath during winter— a winter that would never come into these lands.

There wasn't even anything inside the tower; it was like a hollow shell with a winding stair that ran up around the inside. Celia's heart was pounding in fear as Elithyon dragged her up behind him, no matter what he'd said. What if he forgot by the time they got upstairs? She'd tried to be ready in her mind for her wedding night, but she'd hoped anyway that maybe Gorthan would let her have a few weeks at least, if she asked, to know him a little, and she'd thought she would have sorcery to protect her against anything really dreadful. But she couldn't be ready for *this*.

The staircase went around seven times until it reached the only floor, and ended in a single chamber that filled the space. There was a low wooden bed that seemed very much like the palace itself, only made of thinner branches. It also stood on a platform raised a few inches above the ground, and was lavishly dressed with bedclothes of embroidered silk, with filmy bedcurtains draped around it from the ceiling beams overhead. There was no fire and not even a hearth to light one upon; there were no candles, just shining round lanterns hanging all over from the ceiling at different heights, some of thin paper and some of metal pierced with patterns to let the light gleam out.

Elithyon let her go and went to a pair of doors in the side of the wall and flung them wide onto open air and a world of treetops, a thousand different kinds, vines entangling even the upper branches, and the moon hanging brilliant above, making the leaves silver. He turned and smiled at her, hard and glittering, and said, "I wish you joy of *your* wedding night, Princess," and went out and slammed the door behind him.

Celia sat down on the bed in a gasp of relief and shut her eyes a moment. Then she pushed herself up and went to the huge window and looked out. The great courtyard stood below, empty and deserted, except for the sparkles of the gleambugs and glimmering shapes of sunfish moving deep down in the pools of water. In the time it had taken Elithyon to bring her upstairs, great sheets of ivy had climbed up the tower walls outside, and Celia reached out to try and tug on some of the vines, to see if they might hold her weight. But they drew back from her fingers, and the floor at the edge of the window *shifted* a little underneath her foot, as if it would have liked her to fall out. She pulled back; she wasn't in any hurry to leap from her tower like Eislaing had.

There was a large hanging chair near the window, panels woven of thin reeds and the joining parts made of silken cloth hung from the rafters, heaped inside with many cushions. She went and sat down inside the slightly unsettling swinging cocoon of it and took the bread out of her pocket: she'd gotten nine pieces, which all did still look like bread. She was hungry, but she didn't know when she'd get any more food, so she took one of the cushion covers off and put eight of her pieces inside, and ate only one. And then for lack of any other ideas, she went and lay down on the bed still in her gown and went to sleep; she was too tired and frightened to think of anything at all to do.

In the morning, she jerked up in bed with the curtains held open and Elithyon staring at her in baffled anger, as if he hadn't expected to find her there. He glared at her, and then looked at the window and back, and snarled at her, "Do you think I have made a false oath, then? You imagine that you *could* win my heart?"

"What did you think I'd do?" she said, edging back as far as she could against the pillows. "Throw myself out the window?" But even as she spoke, looking at his seething frustration, she realized that he *had* thought just that. He'd expected her to follow along with Eislaing's story—to *finish* Eislaing's story, with its mirror image: the princess of Prosper driven to her death by the summerlings, the vengeance that he'd agreed to take in place of the war. It hadn't even occurred to him that she'd do anything else, as long as he played out Sherdan's part, by refusing to love her.

He looked at the window again. Celia said, desperately, before he could decide to throw her out himself, "Sherdan didn't *betray* Eislaing! He just didn't love her *yet*—"

Elithyon whipped back, blazing up with brilliant rage all over again. "And once more you try and trick me with the same foul lies, even though they have failed you every time," he said. "The roots of the trees drank her blood and her tears. Do you think they would refuse to tell me the truth of what my sister suffered? How the Betrayer took her from her wedding feast to a foul, low tavern, where he drank and amused himself with his companions, and took himself a slatternly serving-wench to enjoy before her face, leaving Eislaing to wait for his pleasure afterwards, all to teach her that he meant to be the master of a miserable slave, and not the husband of an honored queen?"

And it was true. As soon as Celia heard the words, she knew that of course it was true. Sherdan hadn't had his mother's sorcery. He'd only been a mortal king, and he'd been forced to marry a great lady with magic of her own and a dangerous man at her back, and he'd resented being made to feel small beside her. So he'd insulted her in what he'd thought was a safe and petty way, the way a mortal lord could insult his wife with impunity, to make himself feel more powerful, and he *hadn't* expected her to throw herself out the window. And when she'd chosen to die instead of staying trapped in a loveless alliance, he'd lied to everyone else about what he'd done, so no one would blame him for the war. Just the way Gorthan and the king were surely lying to Father and everyone in Prosper right now about what they'd done with *her*.

Elithyon stood seething another moment, and then he said, "I gave an oath: nothing to be done to you, but what was done to her. If you have so little pride, cling to life as long as you wish. But you will never leave this room again, save the way she left *her* wedding chamber. This I vow to you as well." He turned and stalked from the room, and as he left, the wall closed up tight behind him.

NO ONE CAME INTO THE room the rest of the day. Behind a hanging curtain of thin living vines, as thin as embroidery silk with small green knots tied at intervals, Celia found a beautiful washstand with a mirror so clear that she could have counted her own eyelashes. It showed her no great sorceress, only the face of a frightened girl, with her carefully dressed hair fallen down around her ears, and her heavy gown snagged and crumpled. She managed to wriggle her arms out and twist the gown around her body so she could snap the tiny threads sewing her in, enough of them to shove it all down along with her stays and climb out in just her linen shift, relieved.

There was a washbasin and a jug of summer make on the washstand, both made of the gold that was as hard as steel. As she finished fighting her way out of her gown, it started raining—a brief thrumming downpour so strong that she could fill up the jug for the trouble of holding it out the window and bringing it back inside, in almost a single movement. She filled the washbasin up and drank the jug dry, the water sweet, and ate one piece of her precious store of bread, and then she grimly tried to find something in the room that she could use to cut off her finger, so she could get the imprisoning ring off.

The jug and washbasin were too thick, with carefully blunted edges. She tried to smash the mirror, but even when she threw the jug at it as hard as she could, it only clamored with a sound like bells and didn't even show a mark. The living wood of the bed was smooth and rounded, and when she tried to break off a piece, it only slipped out of her hands. She climbed up on it to try and reach one of the lanterns, but they were too high above her head.

She was about to drag over the washstand and tip it onto the bed so she could climb onto it, and reach them, when she heard horns blowing outside the window. She went and looked down to see the court assembled below again: no feast tables, just Elithyon sitting on his throne upon a dais before the palace, flanked by summer knights, waiting as if to receive visitors. Her tower prison stood to one side of the court, so she could see their faces clearly. Across from him, the trees had arranged themselves into a wide lane, and wonder filled Celia: a great blue-eyed shaihul was coming down the path with pale feathery iridescent scales in a thousand shades of purple and green—

a creature that was half legend even to most summerlings, and held a sign of good fortune whenever one appeared.

The shaihul padded into the courtyard, the tips of its talons clicking on the flagstones, and went all the way up to the throne. "Be most welcome in our court, noble Ali-mathisa," Elithyon said, inclining his head, as warm and gracious as if he'd never felt a drop of hate. "You honor us with your presence. Let us see you refreshed, you and your companion. Eager am I to know what cause has brought you hence."

The shaihul gave a great snorting noise and shook its heavy maned head and answered in a voice like wind blowing in the trees, "Welcome me not, Prince of Endless Summer. I have borne my companion to the heart of your realm in payment of a life debt owed, for the destruction of the vile wyrm Ingrunsir, and the wind whispers that I have brought the doom of many a valiant knight of your realm."

Elithyon was frowning, but he said, "Still I would make you welcome, Alimathisa, and trust in the valor of my knights. But let your companion name himself, and his purpose in coming here."

The knight swung off the shaihul. His back was to her, but as he took off his helm, Celia caught her breath at the familiar movement. She almost called out, but before she could, Elithyon laughed, a ringing sound. "Why, this is no sorrow you have brought me, Alimathisa, but a doubled joy. The Knight of the Woven Blade is a welcome guest to my court indeed." He rose and stepped down the stairs from his throne, holding out both his hands. "Long have I desired to feast you again, Sir Argent, since last we parted at the summer games; all my court are eager to hear more of the deeds that have rung so bright in song throughout my realm. You will sit beside me at table—"

He paused, because he'd reached the bottom step, and Argent wasn't reaching for his hands. Argent said, harshly, "Did you know?"

Elithyon went still, looking him in the face. "What is there for me to have known?"

"Did you know that she's my sister?" Argent said, and Elithyon stiffened. He didn't answer. "Where is she?"

"Argent!" Celia called then, and Argent turned and looked up towards her. He didn't look much older than the last time she'd seen him. He'd been in the Summer Lands the whole time. But he looked so different anyway, as if the strangeness from that last terrible night when he'd left had come to settle down for good inside his face. He'd become even more beautiful, but with the hardness of a statue carved out of stone in a crypt. There was a downturning at the corners of his mouth, where there had always been a lurking smile.

But when he saw her, he smiled anyway, a little softness coming back, and he said, "It's all right, Celie. Don't worry. I'm here," and he sounded almost just like himself, if you didn't know him well enough to hear the effort that it took him to sound cheerful.

Her eyes were smarting with tears. "Argent, I'm sorry," she said. "I'm so sorry. I tried to find you. I was going to come and find you—"

"Silence," Elithyon said, and Celia's voice died in her throat as if someone had put a hand over her mouth.

Argent turned back to face him. "Will you give her to me?"

"Never," Elithyon said sharply. "She is forfeit to the Summer Lands, in return for Eislaing given to the mortal world."

But a low murmuring was going around the court, uneasy, and Elithyon was frowning himself. Summer lords showed their honor by *granting* boons, and they hated to refuse the request of any guest, much less an honored one, and especially one that had done them any kind of service. He threw a savage, glittering glance up at her, in the tower, and then he turned back to Argent. "For the sake of the great deeds you have done, and the evils you have righted in my realm," Elithyon said, sounding as if the words were being pulled out one by one from between his teeth, "I will have her shown small mercy, for in justice, that was not *denied* Eislaing; she simply had too much pride and courage to accept it. The sorceress will be given food and drink, so long as she chooses to take them, and she may live out as many of her mortal days as she wishes. Ask me for nothing more. Your king surrendered her to us full willing."

"My father didn't," Argent said.

Elithyon paused, looking into Argent's face, and narrowed his eyes as if he'd spotted a weakness in his armor. "You have no father," he said, with sudden certainty, and straightened, a look of relief coming into his face, even as Argent flinched back from him a little. "You have no father," Elithyon repeated, with an air of satisfaction. "You have cast him off, for just cause, and she is no kin of yours anymore, for you share no mother's blood. No honor binds you to her cause, and you have no claim to act on her part."

Argent stood a moment, his face rigid with a ghost of remembered pain and anger, and then he said, "I'm not here for *honor*." He stepped back a pace from Elithyon and drew off his gauntlet. He said, "My name is Argent, son of Veris, and I've come for my sister Celia. Bring her to me, or let any lord or knight who would bar my way stand forth and meet me, if he has the courage," and he flung it at Elithyon's feet, the metal ringing against the stones.

"Argent, no!" Celia cried in horror, even as the gasp of thrilled shock went up all around the court. He'd offered an open challenge to every summer knight who chose to face him, and the only difference between that and trying to fight his way to her alone through Elithyon's entire army was that he'd get to fight them one by one, so it would take longer until they killed him.

Elithyon raised his head from the gauntlet to look at Argent. His eyes were so brilliant green, they were almost glowing, and he breathed three times before he spoke again. "For the sake of the injury I have unwitting done you, I will forget the challenge you have made," he said. "Take up your gauntlet and go in peace."

"And let you keep my sister?" Argent said. "No."

Elithyon stood glowering another moment, and then he said icily, "So be it. What knights of my court will take up the challenge?"

There was almost a crash as all six of the summer knights standing by the throne lunged for the gauntlet at once, and others were pouring into the courtyard on all sides, a hundred of them or more, all their faces gone even more inhumanly beautiful, alive with the dreadful joy of their eagerness to be the one to spill Argent's blood, and Celia put her face in her hands in horror. But only for a moment. Then she was up and going for the washstand, even more desperately than before.

She didn't stop to watch the fighting. She could hear too much of it: the formal insults offered to Argent's honor, the threats of how horribly he'd die, and she knew from all her favorite stories that those threats would come true if his opponent managed to disarm him instead of killing him on the field. The ringing clash and scrape of swords came clearly through the window, but even that sound became musical, here in the Summer Lands. She tried not to listen, struggling to heave the heavy washstand onto the bed, but she let it go to slide down with a thump and dashed back to the window in a panic when she heard the choked gurgling cry, and her heart didn't stop beating itself frantically against the walls of her chest even when she saw Argent standing, his sword dipped in red, and the summer knight lying dead at his feet.

By the tenth fight, she'd stopped running to the window every time. She'd gotten the washstand onto the bed, and she'd pulled down all the lanterns that she could reach, now left sprouting around the floor like glowing mushrooms, but none of them had a sharp edge, and their light wasn't even fire, just magic. She put down the last one, and then she looked at the washstand itself; she dragged it to the edge of the bed, and partway off, and when it was teetering back and forth on the edge, she gripped the marble top with just her ring finger around it, the rest of her fingers tucked tight out of the way against it, and then she used her other hand and tugged it to come sliding off towards the ground.

But all the work had been for nothing; the washstand smashed down with her finger in between, just the way she'd hoped, but there wasn't any pain: she wriggled her finger out, and it wasn't even bruised. She stared at it, and then she picked up the jug and just tried bashing it down on her finger, and then on her whole hand: it didn't hurt at all. *Nothing done to her but what was done to Eislaing,* Elithyon had sworn, and Celia realized dismally that nothing in the tower he'd made was going to hurt her, even if she wanted it to.

She threw the jug against the wall and sat down in a heap on the bed and took a pillow and let herself put her head against it and let out a muffled howl of frustration.

Then she did go to the window. Argent was fighting a summer knight who looked like he was half a troll, head and shoulders taller, with a blade as wide as an axe head. She sucked in a sharp breath as Argent had to dive away from a swing, and the summer knight charged after him and swung his blade over and down, but Argent rolled in towards him and stuck a knife into the knight's armor right at the joint below the knee, and then shoved the other leg out from under him, while the momentum of the swing was still going. The troll-knight gave a howl of pain and fell heavily onto his face, and Argent got up behind him and stabbed his sword straight down through the knight's back, and the knight gave a shudder and lay still.

The bodies of twelve other summer knights already lay in a row along the side of the courtyard, draped with red silk and garlanded with vines blooming with pale blue flowers. Argent jerked his blade up and out and stepped back, his shoulders heaving with breath, and four other summerlings came and took the knight's body and carried it reverently to the side to join the horrible line. Argent took his helm off. He was panting heavily, almost trembling a little, and his hair was plastered down to his head with sweat. Celia put her hands over her mouth, tears springing to her eyes. He *couldn't* keep fighting like that for much longer, and the ranks of summer knights waiting to face him had barely been thinned.

But Elithyon had been watching the whole time from his throne, flanked by a rapt audience of summerlings; many of them were applauding, even cheering, as if they'd all forgotten the purpose of the challenge, or were simply overwhelmed by admiration, and Elithyon himself looked as though he would have liked to join in. When the thirteenth knight was borne off the field, Elithyon looked at Argent and then stood up and abruptly announced, "The sun grows high; the next challenge must wait for the heat of the day to pass," and as if he'd given the sun a nudge, it was rising over the trees and blazing heat down into the courtyard as he spoke. "Let all the challengers be given refreshment."

A murmuring swelled through the court, but not of the objections that his people might sensibly have made to Elithyon giving an enemy more chances to kill them. Instead the summerlings all seemed *pleased* by their prince's graciousness, even the other knights who were waiting for their chance to fight. A cool breeze came suddenly blowing out of the trees, and ruffled through Argent's hair and left it smooth and dry and curling again, as if even the forest approved, and a flock of summerling servants went hurrying eagerly towards him, offering him a cup of water to drink, guiding him to a pavilion standing in a small shady grove of trees.

Celia's heart was still beating with fear; she felt like a condemned prisoner with a brief stay of execution granted. She sat down heavily on the cool, low bed and then slowly stretched out and fell into a half-drowsing sleep herself.

But after the sun dipped below the trees on the other side of the forest, the fighting started again. Argent killed another thirteen knights before Elithyon called another halt for the night. Argent was led to the pavilion again, and came out bathed and in fine summerling feasting garb, and was taken to the tables; Elithyon had him seated by his side, and even poured his cup full and served him from the platters with his own hands, showing him all the grace that a summerling host could offer. But Argent only ate steadily through the food and didn't look at him. At the end of the feast, as they all rose, Elithyon burst out in frustration, "You have done great honor to your blade, but you must see that soon you will fall. Will you not withdraw your challenge and be named a guest-friend of my court, welcome to come and go, and see for yourself that the sorceress lives yet?"

Argent said only, "No," and turned to look up at her

window and smiled, before he strode away to the pavilion they'd given him. She could see him in silhouette inside, a light glowing as he sharpened his sword and oiled his armor. Below, Elithyon stood watching his shadow too, with the unhappy, half-wincing expression of a man watching a priceless vase teetering on the edge of a shelf, about to be smashed to pieces. When Argent finished and lay down to sleep, the light softly faded and then went out, and Elithyon turned and glared up at her before going away into the palace, as if he blamed *her* for it all.

Most of the summerlings had drifted away to sleep already, but a few of them wandered into the woods and the gardens, and from her high window, Celia heard two different summerling musicians softly singing to themselves as they worked on rival versions of a lament for the Knight of the Woven Blade, the greatest knight in all the world, who had taken up a hopeless challenge to try and avert the vengeance of the Summer Prince, with a line for every knight he'd met in battle, trying out rhymes for different numbers of the fallen, guessing how many would die before Argent was killed himself.

She listened with her face pressed against her knees, and when at last the last of the musicians had fallen silent, she got up and went to stand at the wide-open window. She looked out straight ahead and tried to pretend that the edge wasn't there. Just one step, and a short fall, and it would be over. Argent wouldn't have anything to keep fighting for, and Elithyon would be glad to let him go. And maybe Argent would have to live out his life in the shadow of the curse she'd left on him, but at least he would live.

And then—Argent would leave the Summer Lands and go back to Father and tell him and Roric what had happened. And they would kill Gorthan and the king, and find some way to lure Elithyon back out of the Summer Lands and kill him, too, and avenge *her* death. That *was* a better story than just living miserably in the power of a proud, cruel man, who was determined to only ever say *no* when you asked him to care. Eislaing hadn't been stupid, after all.

Except that Celia knew how that story ended: in a century of war and sorrow. After her father and her brothers had avenged her, what summer lord would decide that Elithyon's murder had to be avenged in turn, for the trick that had broken the peace? And how many people would *he* slaughter?

She looked down into the pale marble courtyard. There weren't any bloodstains left on the ground; all of them had vanished. All those summer knights dead, and the summerlings weren't angry about a single one of them, because they'd died with honor. They were making songs about Argent killing them, and more knights were lining up eagerly, thinking nothing of the risk of death next to the chance to be part of a truly glorious story. The same way they thought nothing of the people they killed every summer in Prosper. Those people didn't have stories that lived after them. They were just ordinary people: farmers and bakers and weavers, shepherds and millers. They lived and died unseen by the world, forgotten without ever being known by anyone. Anyone except the people who cared for them, the people they cared for.

And the kings of Prosper didn't think about the ordinary people of Prosper any more than the summerlings did, with much less excuse, because they *did* want to live. King Morthimer had been handed a victory in the summer war, and all he'd thought about was making sure that Father didn't take his throne. Likely he hadn't *wanted* the war to end, Celia realized, thinking about it now. The lords of Prosper couldn't afford to squabble amongst themselves when there was a war going. If one of them grew too powerful, the king could just put them in a keep that would be easily overrun, and so what if three villages were slaughtered afterwards?

And surely Elithyon hadn't even really wanted to win the war himself. He'd wanted to keep avenging Eislaing, over and over. As long as he still had to avenge her, she'd stayed in his mind, in his memory, a story that wasn't finished yet. He'd only really invaded Prosper after Father had started defeating his lords decisively, killing so many summerlings, and threatening to force an ending that Elithyon couldn't live with.

Celia wanted that story to end. She didn't want to be

the next chapter, the cause of another round of senseless war. But the only other ending she could write was the one where Argent died trying to save her, on the blade of the thirty-ninth or forty-third or seventy-first summer knight, and she did step off the tower afterwards, instead of starving slowly to death. Then no one else would ever know the truth. Father might guess that Gorthan was lying about the summerlings kidnapping her away from him, but he wouldn't be able to do anything about it, so he'd go home and turn his face to the wall and die, with the two children he'd cared about gone forever. Gorthan and Elithyon would both be crowned, and likely enjoy long and prosperous reigns, reaping the rewards of the summer peace made on the backs of her family.

Celia was her father's sensible daughter, but she was also a descendant of the kings who'd been proud enough to keep a war going just to hang on to their thrones. She'd once swelled with a rage and agony furious enough to make sorcery with, and the story she really wanted was to live, and get out of this tower, and use her sorcery to tear Gorthan and Elithyon both into little pieces. It was their fault, the whole war was their fault: Gorthan and his father following in Sherdan's footsteps, and Elithyon chasing after his own hungry vengeance, with all the same selfishness and pride. She wanted them *dead*, not satisfied and crowned with power; and if she couldn't kill them herself, she did want someone else to kill them.

But she had a second brother. And if she did save the peace, Roric would get the same chance she'd be giving all those other people of Prosper: to make a family that could grow in peace. Roric would take that chance and use it. He'd marry, and have children, and he'd love them all. And he wouldn't avenge Celia, but he'd *remember* her instead. She saw it as clearly in her mind as if she were there: Roric and his wife and children, all together in the warm, glowing sitting room in Todholme Castle, and he'd tell them stories about the sister he'd loved, and who had loved him.

Celia took one step and then another back from the edge. She had promised to care, and she would keep her promise. She'd care about Roric, and she'd care about the people of Prosper, and she'd even care about the summerlings, and give them a chance to write new stories of their own.

BUT IT WAS A HARD choice to make, and harder all the next day, watching Argent fighting one summer knight after another, knowing that she could save his life with a single step over that edge. It would have been easier not to watch, but she'd spent so many days in the stands at Todholme watching him fight that she could see the fighting in her head just from the sound. And by then the summerlings were all applauding wildly after every match, and catching their breath in horrified gasps whenever Argent was in the worst danger, so even if Celia hadn't watched, she would have known every time he was almost about to die.

Instead the only thing that made it easier was Elithyon's growing unhappiness. In the thirteenth match of the morning, Argent fought a knight who had two swords that turned into four and then six, wielded in arms that came springing out of his shoulders like mirror images, and made a whirling cloud of death all around him as a shield. Argent couldn't come at him, and every time he tried, the summer knight answered as quick as lightning, his swords darting in and out. He drew first blood, and second blood, carving slashes through Argent's mail on both his arms, to cries of horror, and then twice more on each of his thighs, blood streaming like thin banners as Argent twisted away, just barely avoiding a mortal blow.

Even as Celia almost cried out to say she'd jump, to stop it, Elithyon lurched up from his throne as if *he* meant to protest, but before either of them could say anything, Argent had continued the movement and come up from under that swinging blade close in to the other knight's body, so close inside his guard they were almost in an embrace, driving a dagger up beneath his ribs.

Argent let the knight slide off him to the ground. His head was hanging with fatigue, and blood was still trickling down into puddles around his feet, and dripping from his wrists. Elithyon didn't even have to declare the halt before the summerlings were already hurrying to Argent with fine bandages of pure undyed silk, but he sent his own cupbearer to bring him a flagon from inside the palace, and from it he filled a drinking horn to the brim with a drink that glowed with shimmers of gold and silver, and carried it to Argent himself. When Argent drank it, the red stains stopped spreading through the wraps. Elithyon stood looking at him and said, "Withdraw your challenge, and the sorceress will live out her mortal days in comfort; she will have food and drink befitting of her rank, and I will even have servants attend her, to see to her needs," as if he were at a negotiating table, bargaining for Argent's life, and he sounded as desperate to save it as Celia felt herself.

That didn't make it easier to watch Argent straightening up to hand back the cup, and saying steadily, "No," before he turned and went to his pavilion, to get ready to keep fighting his way to the death ahead of him. But it did make it easier for Celia to forgive Elithyon when he bowed his head in misery at Argent's back. His sorrow cooled the hot resentment inside her like a breath of autumn air through the windows of Castle Todholme, and when he turned and glared up at her in a rage, his fists clenched, she didn't glare back at him. She looked at him and didn't try to hide her own grief: a terrible fate they had to endure together.

His own fury quenched as he stared up at her, as if he saw something in her face he didn't understand. He sat with grim resignation all the next day, and after Argent went to rest with seventy-eight summerling knights dead by the side of the courtyard, higher than any of the song-makers had guessed after the first night, Elithyon came up the tower stair and burst into her chamber and stood over her where she sat curled on the stones by the edge of the window, watching Argent oiling his mail for the next day.

"Do you imagine even he can win your freedom?" he said savagely. "Never have I seen such valor, but it cannot bring him victory in this challenge. He may slay a hundred of my knights, but what good will it do you? A hundred hundred more will come forth willingly to face him in the court. End this. I will let you speak to him. Tell him that you wish him to accept the bargain. You will have food and drink, and service—"

He stopped there a moment, but then in the pavilion, Argent got up to put his sword on the rack, and the step he took was limping, even though Elithyon had given him another silver-gold draught at the end of the night. Elithyon saw it, and he clenched his fists by his sides and bit out, "You will have more chambers here in the tower, garments befitting a queen as well, and each night among your dreams you will walk among the gardens. Will this not satisfy you better than to sit here and cower, clinging to a miserable existence that will last you only long enough to wither the most shining flower of knighthood that ever my realm has seen?"

She stood up and faced him and held out her hand. "Take off the ring, you with your ten thousand knights at your back, before you call *me* a coward."

He glared at her over it, his jaw tight. "You are determined, then, to see him die for your sake?" he said in cold disgust. "To waste such courage and strength and honor, for no reason?"

And she knew it wasn't any use, but Elithyon had known the same thing, and he'd tried anyway; she had to bargain for Argent's life too, if she had any chance at all. So she said, "Let me tell him that I don't want to be avenged. If he'll agree to go, and forget about me, I'll jump." Only even as she said it, she couldn't help but think of the curse, the curse that had so twisted Argent's life. If she was dead, it would weigh on him forever. But she couldn't help asking anyway.

Elithyon stared at her, bewildered. He said, "*Not* avenge you—" and stopped, as if he couldn't make any sense of the request.

"Argent won't die for *my* sake," Celia said. "I'll be dead a minute after he is. But then this war you've made will be over for good, and the people of Prosper will be able to sleep in summer. And that's worth dying for. But *he* doesn't have to die, if he'll just let it end here—"

"No," Elithyon said, interrupting her. He'd drawn back from her as she spoke, his face going blank with the dismay of someone realizing he'd misunderstood an enemy, and now he broke in and shook his head almost fiercely. "No." He stopped a moment, and said in almost a whisper, "Eislaing too loved her people, and the quiet folk. But if she had asked such a thing of *me*, to let her die un-avenged, forgotten, could I have granted her plea? It would have been only a bitter sorrow to know that, in her final hour, I caused her any grief. Why should you wound him so?" He turned and left her in the room, and she didn't try to argue with him. She knew that he was right.

But she also knew, before the end of the next morning, that it was Argent's final day, and hers. He'd recovered after the night's rest, but his strength slipped away a little more quickly. And after she'd watched him fight and kill thirteen more summer knights, she ate an extra piece of bread, even though she'd only been letting herself have one each day. She was hungry, and there wasn't any sense in suffering any more than she was going to anyway.

The summerlings knew, also. They'd stopped applaud-ing after the victories; they were all silent now instead. When the midday halt came, the servants went to Argent and tended him gently, speaking in low voices as they guided him back to his pavilion. He'd been wounded five times that morning. Elithyon watched from his throne with his face hopeless, and even looked up at her in misery instead of rage, as if he wanted to see someone sharing his grief. She met his gaze; she wanted the same thing. She was so glad that it would hurt him when Argent died. She was glad to think that he'd have to remember this as the end of the story he'd written for his sister: not a triumph, but a tragedy.

And then the sun crept over the sky, much too quick, and Argent came back to the courtyard. He fought and killed nine knights, but the ninth one put a blade through his side, front to back, even as he fell, and afterwards Argent sank to his knees in the courtyard, pressing a hand to the wound. Elithyon jerked a gesture and sent servants in to dress the wound, and let his head fall into his hand. Around the courtyard, all the summer knights who'd been so eager to fight before were edging back instead, as if none of them wanted to be the one to come in and strike what all of them could see would be a mere executioner's blow.

Celia had stood up, her hands clenched, involuntarily. She looked at the edge, and thought again about jumping. But after the wound had been bound up tight, Argent looked up at her and smiled again, more familiar than he had been ever since the day he'd first ridden away from home to go to the summer games. Lightness and ease had come back into his face; the hard desperate grip he'd had on himself suddenly unclenched. "It's all right, Celie," he said. "Don't worry," and she understood at last what he was telling her. This was his own way around the curse: a way to die for love, instead of glory. Something that was worth dying for, to him.

She did start crying then, because she knew that meant she couldn't jump, after all, even in the last moment. Because that would be worse for him than if he died. This was his last chance, his only chance. No one else could love him, that he could love. He'd chosen, the same way she had. Tears were running down her face, but she also made herself smile back at him, and she said, "I love you," to let him know she understood.

Argent bent down, carefully, and picked up his sword. "I'm ready," he told Elithyon, and then one of the summerlings at the edge of the court cried out urgently, "Your Highness, look there through the trees—a visitor comes to your court!"

Elithyon sat up in flaring relief and said, "We must halt the challenge for the nonce, that we may welcome our guest," a reprieve she thought he was granting to himself, more than to either of them.

But then she caught her breath as Roric came into the court and bowed his red-capped head, still dressed as a song-spinner. When Elithyon asked, he said, "I've come to offer my poor skills to amuse the Summer Prince and his court, if you'll have me," and Elithyon said eagerly, "Play for us, then. Let us hear your finest songs and tales, and you shall feast with my court this night, and for every night so long as you continue."

The servants were already gladly guiding Argent away to his pavilion, and Roric started to pluck a bouncing melody, a simple lighthearted children's song going in a round, and with that going beneath his voice, he started to tell the summerlings a story—a story of how a group of foolish knights attacked a hill fort of the forest animals, and were driven off by a small army of rabbits with twenty sacks of carrots, three bars of solid brass, nine bolts of good woolen cloth, and ten cartloads of firewood.

It wasn't a story she'd told him before; the account-stories weren't stories to remember, and they always laughed and forgot them even as she told them. But it was *one* of them—a silly story that teetered wildly from one side to the other like a cart being unbalanced with every new number being crammed into it, threatening to tip over into nonsense all the way. They were stories that needed a generous audience, but this story had one, and the summerlings laughed the way that Roric had laughed, willingly, every time the story asked them to, or even just gave them the least excuse, glad to be distracted. When he was done, they applauded as wildly as if he'd sung them the entire Lay of Lethien from memory, and Roric said, "I could do another, if you want," and Elithyon said, "Play on, so long as you can!"

Celia didn't eat another piece of bread that night. Roric told them three more of the silly account-stories, bringing in some of the handful of characters she'd used more often: the clear-eyed vixen, the determined hedgehog, the one brave true knight who turned up to rescue the pack of silly ones from their misadventures whenever she'd gotten them stuck in an impossible corner, and chided them for attacking the kingdom of the forest. The summerlings drank toasts to him out of their drinking horns and laughed more and more with each one, growing giddy with merriment, until the sun went down, and Elithyon gladly called for the feast tables. Argent was seated on his right side, and Roric on his left. Celia didn't think Argent had recognized Roric; he looked as if he barely even saw what was around him, his face remote and lined a little with pain, wan as fresh linen, but he still had that lightness in him, a calm that made him seem almost ethereal, a ship about to slip out with the tide into a morning fog. Elithyon looked only at him, his hands clenched as if on a rope to hold it back.

The next morning, Elithyon asked Roric to keep going, and Roric told them thirteen more stories, each one more or less absurd. When he started to find it hard to invent more numbers, without the account books in front of him, he turned to the summerlings themselves. He said, "And then the lambs opened up the sack that the shepherd had left in his hut, and inside they found forty-two . . ."

and looked around at the audience, beckoning with a hand, until one of the summerlings suddenly shouted out, "Silver arrows!" and Roric went on from there, and after that all the summerlings were truly alive with delight, twenty or more of them calling suggestions every time he held open the door for them to add their own part into the tale, gleeful and congratulated by their companions when their offering was taken.

Only Elithyon paid no attention to the stories. He was still looking at Argent, who was pale and bowing a little over his place with each breath, a hand resting over the wound in his side, even though Elithyon had filled his horn with the silver-gold potion three times the night before. Elithyon gave him another draught in mid-morning, but even that only brought a brief flush of health into his cheeks. Almost at once it faded away again into pallor, and when Elithyon tried to give him another, during the midday rest, Argent held it off and lifted his head, and Celia heard him say, "Haven't I put on enough of a show already?" with a note of impatience in his voice.

Elithyon lurched back as if he'd been struck across the face. He said, "No—*no*—" inarticulate, and Argent paused, looking at him with a slow stirring of surprise rising through the veiling fog of pain and weariness, as if he'd only just noticed that Elithyon—*cared.* His eyes widened, staring at him, and Elithyon stared back, his own face caught with the same understanding, as if he'd just noticed it himself, and for a moment Argent lifted a hand towards him.

But before Elithyon could do anything—before he could choose, to lean in, or to put the hand aside—Argent stopped and said to Elithyon again, slowly, "Will you give me my sister?" like someone putting a foot gingerly out onto a bridge, to see if it would hold his weight.

But Elithyon said faintly, "I have—I have sworn an oath—" with a kind of horror in his voice.

Argent was already letting his hand sink, pulling back to solid ground: the easy, serene calm had returned, even as Celia's eyes were prickling with sorrow. Of course it wasn't enough to break the curse, not when Elithyon would still put honor first. That wasn't anything that Argent would call love. He nodded, unsurprised, and said simply, "Farewell then, Your Highness," and then he pushed himself up from his seat with an effort and walked away from the tables to his pavilion, and inside he began to put back on his mail. The sun had just begun to dip below the trees again, throwing the cool shadows over the palace.

Elithyon looked as if a blade had been put through him from front to back, too, and he just hadn't pulled it out yet. He sat watching Argent's pavilion, his face unmoving and blank, while some of the other summerlings along the tables began to call hesitantly for Roric to give them another tale, glancing to see if Elithyon approved, and some of the summer knights, seeing Argent arming himself, looked at him uncertainly, and a few of them rose, and went to put on their own mail.

Roric had been careful before then not to look up at the tower, but with everyone looking at Elithyon, he flicked his eyes up and caught Celia's. She gave him back a small nod, trying not to hope, as Elithyon jerked beneath the rising murmuring of his court and asked Roric with a desperation bright in his voice, "But I have commanded you to sing as long as you can. Have you no more songs nor tales to share?"

"Well—I do know *one* more, Your Highness," Roric said, with an air of reluctance, "but it's very long—"

"Sing it!" Elithyon said, all the more eager, a chorusing murmur of encouragement joining him from the court.

Roric put on a show of wavering, and then he blurted, "—and I'm afraid it might offend you! Please don't ask me to sing it."

"If that is all, sing without fear," Elithyon said. "I swear to you that you shall suffer no punishment nor retribution."

Roric hesitated again and said, "Do you promise? If I sing it, you won't do any injury to me, or let any of your subjects do one, even if you're very angry? Or to any of my kin?" he tacked on hastily, like an afterthought. "I know a summer prince won't break his oaths."

"Indeed I will not," Elithyon said. "You have my word upon it, spinner. Therefore, sing on!"

There was a heaviness on the court this time as Roric started, as if they all shared in Elithyon's misery, and Celia didn't know if Roric would be able to catch them again. But he didn't tell another one of the account-stories. Instead he started playing a song Celia recognized: it was the tune of "The Foolish Miser," but when he started singing and talking his way through the song, he'd changed the words around a little to make it a lord instead who'd had his jewel stolen, and started looking for it in all the wrong places. In Roric's song, first the lord met an honest baker, who said he hadn't taken the jewel. "So then he killed the baker dead, and tore up all his loaves of bread, but he didn't find his jewel," Roric went on, singing the chorus through twice as he went up and down the tables, and a few of the summerlings started joining in with him the second time, another handful clapping along.

The lord in his song met and murdered an honest potter, and smashed all his vases and his jugs, without any more success. Some more of the summerlings joined in the chorus with Roric that time, and then the lord met an honest shepherd who said he hadn't taken his jewel, and killed him too. "The lord said, 'I swear I'll find my jewel,'" Roric sang, "'if I have to search every ram and ewe,' and he went through them one by one," and Roric paused the music and put a hand to his mouth and said loudly in a false aside, "Baaa-aah!" making it sound deeply distressed. It took a moment, but all the summerlings took his meaning; even Elithyon jerked his eyes away from Argent's pavilion to gawk at him, and the whole court exploded into gales of laughter. When Roric went on, they all chorused with him in delight, "But he didn't find his jewel!"

He had the court with him wholeheartedly, then. Roric kept the song going through ten more honest men and women, all murdered for nothing: a merchant, a butcher, a candlestick maker; a tavern wench, a weaver, a hedge knight, a priest; a cook, a nursemaid, and even a young bride on the way to her wedding. The summerlings had laughed at all the others, but they gasped in indignation when the lord killed her and hunted through her dower chest, and the whole court was still murmuring when at the last the lord met a fine city man, who kept one hand in his pocket. Roric sang, "The city man furrowed his brow and said, 'Is your jewel agleam in shades of green?' And the lord cried out, 'It is!' The city man furrowed his brow and said, 'Is your jewel the finest ever seen?' And the lord cried out, 'It is!'" Roric made a great burst of strumming and then spoke for the city man in a mock whisper. "'Why my lord—I know who took your jewel!'"

All the summerlings were leaning forward in eagerness as Roric continued, "'I saw such a jewel just this day, a sly fox holding it on the way, taking it to bury far away, in the hillside over the ridge.' And the city man pointed the lord to the hill, with the hand that wasn't in his pocket." The lord thanked the city man and praised him for the first honest man he'd found, and he ran to the field and started digging in every gopher hole and rabbit burrow he could find. "And the city man strolled on down to the market town, to have a fine green jewel set into a crown, while the lord went on digging in the mud," Roric finished.

The summerlings all applauded riotously for a long time, many of them throwing jeweled ornaments and summer gold at Roric's feet. Elithyon himself was smiling again, mirthfully, the coming sorrow slipped away from him entirely for a glad moment; he said, "Well, songspinner, why should this song have offended me?"

Roric said, "It's called 'The Summer War,'" and all the summerlings stopped laughing.

After a moment, Roric added into the heavy silence, "It's the song that everyone's singing in Prosper about the war. You made peace with the heirs of the Betrayer, and they still rule the kingdom, and all you did was kill a lot of people who had nothing to do with it at all."

The summerlings were deep in shock, darting looks at Elithyon, who was sitting rigidly, his hands clenched on the arms of his throne, a rising storm about to burst. But before he could say anything, Argent ducked out of his pavilion, wearing his armor. He looked to see that the performance was over, and the sun wasn't quite down, yet.

He reached back in for his woven blade, and then he went straight to stand in the center of the courtyard, in the challenge ring. His eyes were too-brilliant in his wan face, but he still wore the serene look, almost smiling, and he didn't even notice the appalled silence of the court at first, until he'd stood in the middle of it for long enough to feel it lapping against him like a tide against a shore, and then he stirred, and looked up a little puzzled at Elithyon.

Elithyon looked down at Argent, and then jerked and looked over at the summer knights ranged against the side of the courtyard, already gathered to kill him. Memory swept over him, and the storm broke instead. He gasped, and said, his voice thick with agony, "May Eislaing's shade forgive me, the song is true. I have taken the wrong vengeance." He put his face into his hands with a cry of grief.

The court was silent with him, sharing the sharp point of sorrow, and they all glared with sudden furious hate when Roric broke in on the silence and said, "But it's over now. You gave your word."

Elithyon raised his head to look down at him. His jaw went murderously tight with anger, and he said through lips that barely moved, "I gave my word that no harm would come to you, song-spinner, and wise you were to demand it. Otherwise you would not leave this court alive, for the insult you have given me this day—even if you have but shown me my own error. You will be no witness to my sorrow. Go forth from my lands at once, and well you should fear returning. You are a strange fool, to dare come to mock a prince in his own court."

"That's not why I came," Roric said.

He'd come to stand next to the challenge ring, before the throne, and as he spoke, Argent's brows began to furrow. He turned and looked into Roric's face under the red cap and said, "*Roric?*" in sudden bewilderment.

Roric looked up at Argent. He was a head shorter, and they didn't look alike at all, but a ray of late sun came dappling through the trees onto them, and up in the tower, Celia could see their shadows stretched out stark on the pale flagstones of the courtyard, facing each other with the matching long narrow slope of their father's nose in both their profiles. "Roric," Argent said again, his face brightening a little more. "*You* came for Celie, too," and smiled down at him.

Celia could see Roric's face working a little with the urge to fall into the old scowling lines. Of course Argent hadn't ever realized that Roric was jealous of him; Argent hadn't paid enough attention, too busy trying to fill all his longing with the sword, trying to be fit to be their father's son and heir. But he'd also never been angry or jealous in return. To him, Roric had always just been his little brother.

And of course that would only annoy Roric more, but Roric's face wasn't used to scowling anymore, and Argent looked too distant, pallid as a ghost, and instead of scowling, Roric just grimaced briefly, and then he said, almost gently, "Yes. I came, too."

Elithyon slowly stood up from his throne, staring down at them both. Roric turned back to face him, and said, "You promised. No harm to me or any of my kin. Not me, and not my sister—and not my brother," and the whole court drew a united gasp of horror and understanding, seeing too late the way that Roric had snared Elithyon in a woven net of oaths that couldn't all be kept.

Elithyon stood motionless at the top of the dais. Celia wondered what would it mean, for the ruler of the summerlings to break an oath? It had never happened in a single one of the summer stories that she'd ever read. There wasn't a single murmur, a single whisper of wind or birdsong, as if all the endless Summer Lands now hung on his breath, on his next words. She couldn't help but think that maybe it did, and whichever way he turned, the whole realm might come tumbling down.

And then Elithyon looked down at Argent, and suddenly a light came dawning into his face, almost the same kind of relief that Celia had seen in Argent's. Elithyon came down from the dais, and Roric half put out an arm towards Argent, backing away a little warily, but Elithyon didn't advance on them. He stopped, standing before the challenge square, and said in a ringing voice, "Come forth and arm me."

A low murmuring of something between relief and

fear went around the court even as the royal servants came forward. In a grand, stately procession they armed Elithyon in one glorious piece of summer make after another— a shining coat of mail made of gilded steel that folded over his shoulders, a gleaming vest made of narrow plates sewn over green silk, a shoulder girdle with pauldrons of gold enameled with beetle-iridescence, greaves and boots and gauntlets of steel washed with silver and gold, and from his shoulders they hung a cape of green that seemed half silk and half leaves, clasped in gold again. They brought him a round shield of wood bound in gold, and a spear whose shaft was a living branch with curling leaves, and the head shining golden.

When they finished, Elithyon said, "My people, hear my command: I will stand as the last challenger, and should the Knight of the Woven Blade prevail, my honor shall be sealed with my death in battle, in defense of my oath; no other need stand in his way. You will let him go into the tower, and bring his sister forth from her chamber by the door. And then let the singer and his kin go forth from our lands without harm, and fulfill my last promise. I charge you only to remember forever the fool's mistake your prince once made, and evade it henceforth. Well I should have known that he who bargains with liars and cheats can gain nothing but shame and misery thereby."

Roric threw a half-surprised look up at Celia, uncertain whether to be glad or not. But her own heart was tumbling down as if she'd taken it in both her hands and dropped it off the tower. The summerlings were all weeping, many of them hiding their faces in their hands, their heads bowed low. Elithyon stepped proudly forward into the ring of challenge and stood facing Argent with his shield lowered and his spear held aside, his guard wide open, inviting in the killing blow. Elithyon's face was exalted with having found a way out of his own trap, but the rest of Argent's serenity, already muddled with confusion, was draining away into horror. He didn't move. Both of them just stood there.

After a long moment, Elithyon frowned and said to him, "Why do you hold your blade? Strike, strike true, and you shall have your sister, in fulfillment of your challenge," as if he thought Argent needed it explained, and then he even smiled at Argent brilliantly and added, "Indeed it comes to me that my own sister told me, chiding me once for my hasty temper, with what now I see was a gift of prophecy, that I was foolish to indulge it, and one day I would be more glad to die than have vengeance for my deepest grief. So it is, for it seems to me now that all my days would have been shadowed without any hope of end, had I watched you fall in my court as the price of my revenge. Better this by far!"

Argent didn't say a word. He only gave a strangled cry of anguish and bowed his head; tears were dripping from his face, down onto his woven blade, tracing along the threaded bands of gold and silver and steel. Roric was looking from him to Elithyon in rising dismay, realizing that he'd snared *both* of them in his trap.

And above, Celia was caught in her own horror and understanding: it was the curse. Argent had struggled his way through all its terms. He'd ridden a shaihul and slain a dragon, he'd become the greatest knight in all the world, and through all of it, he'd never stopped caring about love more. He'd come to save her, to die saving her, for love; he'd met a hundred summerlings in battle, one by one, and never wavered, and at last his courage and strength and skill had brought him to *someone stupid enough to love him again*—

And now the curse would force Argent to *kill* him, for *her sake*. To fulfill the childish, resentful wish of a little girl's heart, to be more important to him than anyone else he might ever meet. To stand between him and a summer lord with shining green eyes who would have asked him to stay, to care.

Tears were pouring down Celia's face. She would so much rather have jumped from the tower herself after all; only that wouldn't work either, because Argent loved *her*, too. He did love her. It would shatter his heart just as much to know that she'd jumped to spare him. How could he ever stay with Elithyon, after that? But if he killed Elithyon now, then he'd never be able to stay with *her*, either. He'd be truly loveless then, forever, either way. There wasn't a way out.

She looked despairing down at her hand, at the ring of cold black steel tight around her finger, locking up the sorcery that she'd wrung out of all this pain in advance. Her own sorrow and rage had only been the first payment, and the rest was now due. And she'd saved it all for nothing, to sit in her belly the way she had to sit in this tower, useless, helpless. She was the one who'd made the curse; she was the one who had to find the way to break it. She'd known that all along. If only she could have done anything at all, she would have known what to do; she was her father's daughter. If she'd had even a drop of sorcery, she would have—

Celia slowly turned her head and looked the other way out the window, towards the open end of the courtyard, where the shaihul was seated in state underneath a great shaded canopy, with a silver bowl of golden wine to drink. But it wasn't drinking at all; it was sunk low on itself, its head resting on its forelegs and its enormous eyes wet and full of sorrow, watching the terrible drama playing out. She called out, "Lord Alimathisa!"

Argent had been starting to raise up his sword, without raising up his head. Roric put out his hand to hold Argent's arm back, and Argent turned, both of them looking up at her. But she was looking at the shaihul, which lifted its head and blinked at her like an owl. "Lord Ali-mathisa," she said, "would you mind coming up here, so if I jump from this tower, I'll land on your back?"

Roric burst out in a squawking awkward burst of laughter, pure relief, and put his fist over his mouth to press it in. The shaihul had pulled its head back into its neck, swelling out an enormous collar of puffed-up feathers, as if it was a little indignant at the idea—but then it got up on its legs and shook itself out, and sprang in a single leap up to the tower. It landed on the wall outside on all four feet, standing just below the window as if the world could turn sideways for it, and bent its head to look inside. Celia lurched back a little; the shaihul had looked much smaller below. Its head filled the entire window, and it blinked its dinner-plate eyes at her a moment before it turned and offered her its back. The distance was more of a step than a jump, but she didn't think anyone was going to quibble; she took a small hop off the ledge and sank through a cloud of feathers to land on its back.

Celia hadn't felt the curse when she'd made it, but she thought she could feel the awful weight of it lifting away from her, left behind in the tower prison as Alimathisa lightly jumped down to the ground, a single bounding leap onto soft enormous paws, and Roric darted forward to help her slide down to the ground.

"There," she said to Elithyon, sliding down with the help of Roric's hand; he'd darted forward to meet her.

"I've left the tower the same way Eislaing did, and none of your oaths are broken, as long as you don't hurt me or my brothers."

Elithyon slowly lowered his spear and shield, almost a little puzzled, or maybe deflated; the solution surely wasn't grand and tragic enough for him. But then he drew a deep breath and said, low, "That I shall not do. But still I cannot let you go—save by breaking the peace between our realms, which you would have died to preserve." And he looked over at Argent, who stared back at him miserably, and maybe he'd found a way to dig up his tragedy after all.

Celia bit her lip, thinking, but before she could come up with anything, a muffled voice said, "Wait." Celia turned around. Some low shrubs were clustered together at the base of the tower, right where the ivy went climbing up, and a knight came pushing his way out of the under-growth, as if he'd been hiding there. He stepped into the courtyard, a hedge knight in an old and rusty suit of armor without a tabard or even a painted sigil to mark his crest: Father.

He took off his helm, and looked around the court-yard, taking all of them in with bright and narrow eyes: his sons, his daughter, and his enemy. Roric had his chin jutting a bit defiantly as Father looked at him. Father didn't say anything, but after a moment, he gave a little nod, the little nod that meant: *Yes, well done.* Roric had never gotten it aimed at him before, but he still recognized it. He swallowed visibly, his hand clenching and unclenching around the neck of his lute.

Every last summer knight in the court had put their hands on the hilts of their blades and was looking around as if they expected an army to suddenly pop out of their own forest at any instant. But Father just came over to Celia and held out his hand; she gave him hers with the coal-black ring, and he turned back with her to Elithyon, who was eyeing him with more than a little wariness himself. "You gave Prosper your sister, a princess of the Summer Lands, and King Morthimer offered you a princess of Prosper in return," Father said. "But my daughter isn't one, and never will be; she's going to be the queen. So take back your ring, and let her go home to be crowned." He paused and looked at Argent, whose eyes were bright with tears as Father finished softly, "And she'll give you her brother to seal the peace, instead."

THE LAST BATTLE OF THE summer war wasn't very long. Father had worked out the king's plot as soon as Gorthan had come out of the grove alone, claiming that Celia had been snatched by the summerlings. Father had pretended to be overcome with fury and said he was going to prepare an assault on the Summer Lands, but instead he'd sent his men riding away to every town along the border, to spread the word of how the king and Crown Prince Gorthan had treacherously given away the power of sorcery to their enemies, and that Grand Duke Veris had bravely gone into the Summer Lands in disguise to save his daughter. By the time they came out again, the word had spread through all of Prosper.

The royal court had been very empty of support by the time Father marched up to the palace with an army greatly swelled by an angry mob of common folk and armed with spears and arrows of summer make. Elithyon couldn't invade again, but that didn't mean he couldn't help. They'd held a parley on the drawbridge with Crown Prince Gorthan, who darted a guilty look at Celia and offered, in a stilted way, to marry her after all.

"No, all in all, I think I'd prefer to just have your throne," Celia said, icily, before Father could even answer. "Your father can keep the title of Grand Duke, and have our northern estates to be your lands, in exchange for the lands of the crown. And if that's not good enough, I'll send both of you to the Summer Lands, and see how much *you* enjoy Elithyon's hospitality. Decide before sunset."

The king chose to quietly leave for the north that same day, with a few hundred armsmen and his remaining family retainers. In the last golden rays of the summer sunset, Celia watched them all riding away from the walls of the royal palace, and then she went inside to sleep luxuriously sprawled out all alone across the enormous royal bed that she'd had moved to a suite on the first floor, from whose window she could have jumped to the ground without even spraining an ankle.

They took the rest of the summer to properly rebuild the old royal palace at the Green Bridge. Many willing hands pulled up weeds and cleared the rotted wood, gathered fallen stones and quarried new blocks and baked new bricks, and mixed a great vat of quicklime mortar, and then Celia stood at the foot of the old collapsed winter towers and used sorcery to raise them all back up to their full height in a single day, stones flying like flocks of mixed birds into their places, from great blocks to little dusty chips left scattered.

And in the outer courtyard they pickaxed up the dark-stained flagstones at the foot of the highest tower, and gently took out the two rows of old dead trees, all of them still bowed over with grief, that once had stood there. The summerlings planted new seedlings in their place, and Elithyon walked among them, speaking to them softly, and overnight they grew into something between an autumn hall and a summerling palace, pillared in living wood, and even before they had finished furnishing it, gleam-bugs were making small stars among the rustling entwined leaves above.

They held the coronation and the wedding on the same day, with a great joyful feasting laid out ready to celebrate, leaping summerling bonfires of colored flames, ringed by beds of coals over which a vast array of wild game and luscious summer fruits sizzled, filling the air with rich roasting smells of a thousand foods that no one in Prosper could remember tasting. The feast tables were laden with cakes and sparkling wine and towering spun-sugar sculptures of castles and dragons that enraptured all the summerlings.

Celia came to the palace driving in an open cart along the royal road, through a throng of common folk. Father had been wary of an assassination attempt, but she'd insisted. As they drove through, she reached out her hands to as many of them as she could reach, to her people, the people she'd chosen to care about, and as if they knew, smiles and cheers met her as they reached back eagerly, calling out blessings for her reign. More of them were looking on, crammed into every balcony and window of the towers, as Father put the crown on her head inside the inner court-yard, and they made such a lusty din of cheering that even the stuffiest of the aristocrats in their cushioned seats on the ground floor darted looks up and thought it only sensible to put on a show of enthusiasm of their own.

Father had escorted the Dowager Marchioness of Travinia to a seat in the front row, with Roric on her other side, wearing the red fox tabard of their house. "She's been telling me stories about every single eligible heiress in the realm," Roric said to Celia in the dancing after, wavering between bewilderment and laughter. "She says she'll host a party to introduce me to all the ones that aren't 'soul-devouring ninnies.'"

But first, once she'd been crowned, Celia went to Argent, sitting on the marchioness's other side. The time they'd taken to rebuild the palace had also been the time they'd taken to let him heal. He finally had some color back in his cheeks, and he was smiling up at her as she held out her hands. He stood with her and they walked together back out of the tower courtyard and into the living hall, and when they came out of it, on the other side of the outer courtyard stood the Summer Palace, as if the courtyards of the two palaces had overlapped. There was somehow room for all the crowding mortal guests, and also for all the summerling court.

Elithyon was waiting for them standing before his own throne with his eyes gleaming like green jewels, in robes of silk, and Celia brought Argent to him and said, "Summer King Elithyon, I bring to you my brother, Sir Argent of the Woven Blade, to be your companion in the Summer Lands, and seal the peace between our people." She turned and kissed her brother's cheek, and then laid Argent's hand in his, and stepped back smiling through tears as they kissed one another with all the trees and vines around them blooming so furiously that the embroidered flowers on their clothes began to lift off the fabric and come alive to join them.

ABOUT THE AUTHOR

NAOMI NOVIK has written the Scholomance trilogy, the novels *Uprooted* and *Spinning Silver*, and the Temeraire series. She is a founder of the Archive of Our Own.

naominovik.com
Facebook.com/naominovik
X: @naominovik
Instagram: @naominovik

ABOUT THE TYPE

This book was set in Baskerville, a typeface de-
signed by John Baskerville (1706–75), an ama-
teur printer and typefounder, and cut for him
by John Handy in 1750. The type became
popular again when the Lanston Monotype
Corporation of London revived the classic
roman face in 1923. The Mergenthaler Lino-
type Company in England and the United
States cut a version of Baskerville in 1931,
making it one of the most widely used type-
faces today.